THE WAKING NIGHTMARES

Serial One: Omnipresence

Book 3

Tales From the Dream Nebula: The Waking Nightmares

Copyright 2023 © M. D. Boncher

1st Edition

Cover Design: Neutronboar

ISBN: 979-8-9881492-2-4 - Paperback

LINKS & SOCIAL MEDIA

If you enjoyed the book, the best thing you can do for an indie author like myself is leave a review from where you purchased the book and any other social media outlets you enjoy. Let others know what you think, including the author. Your reviews are appreciated.

For news on all creative projects of M.D. Boncher, you can find updates, communication and news at Resonant Point:

www.thedreamnebula.com

www.resonantmedia.art

BIBLIOGRAPHY

Wild Adventure Sci-Fi

Tales From the Dream Nebula

01. Dreams Within Dreams
02. Lucid Reality
03. The Waking Nightmares

Dark Epic Christian Fantasy

Akiniwazisaga

A Light Rises in a Dark World
The Inheritance Thieves
Into The High Places

TABLE OF CONTENTS

THE DREAM NEBULA

Long ago, after the 21st century, Earth was conquered by an evil power: Xiao the Eternal. The entire solar system was subsumed into his realm, the Dream Nebula. Every living being was meticulously captured and cataloged by his invasion and placed into suspended animation.

When humanity was released again as Xiao's subjects, reality as they knew it was gone. There were no stars, no inky black vacuum of space. Even the sun was missing. Only the shredded wreckage of planets, moons and asteroids, floating in endless technicolor clouds and perpetual winds, remained.

Time marched on for the subjects of the empire. They painfully rebuilt their cultures like bonsai in Xiao's hands. They shared their vassal nations with mechoids, sentient mechanical beings, new species of uplifted anthromorphs and living AIs called dataoids.

In time, most of humanity obsessed over their lost history. Desires and hearts turned toward rebellion, the overthrow of the Emperor, and freedom.

1.

Warm light poured down over Winston as Puala'Lolo's rotation took him out of the faint shade of the palm tree he had been relaxing under. He snored contentedly in a lounge chair in the early afternoon till the baking sand's heat gently woke him.

He looked off into the seemingly endless distance to the ocean's edge. Bright white local clouds puffed up into little thunderheads like ancient sailing ships, while above them the grandiose clouds of the Dream drifted by in pale pastel pinks, teals and oranges common to its tropical upper layers.

Life here had been a veritable spa as part of his convalescence following their departure from Nova Tortuga. The last few weeks out of the cab at this height of the Dream turned his skin a deep tan. He picked up his Plammer from the small table beside his chair and took a swig. The ice cold sweat felt good in his hand, and the mix of iced tea and lemonade was perfect for his lazy mood.

He paused mid-drink as he saw the long tail of a far off skytrain pulling away from Puala'Lolo, its huge tug pulling hundreds of shimmering containers behind it. Memories of piloting the *Sierra Madre* all over the known Dream came back in a rush. Despite all the bad times, he really missed that simple life. No way back to it now. He'd have to make do with whatever came next.

The thought struck him that this was his first vacation ever, even if it was due to his current cavalcade of suffering. A bitter bubble of memory rose to the surface as he realized he could not share this moment with Val and Emmy.

Had so many things gone wrong in such a short time? Getting blackballed from the only career he knew, then Mother getting him mixed up with gun runners for the rebellion, barely surviving a Black Void event was only the tip of the ice cube it seemed. Rescuing a secret insane asylum and getting brainburned really didn't help either. Then there was Holly. He didn't know whether to laugh, cry, smile or pine for her loss thanks to her messing with his brain with that limbic manipulator of hers.

An ice cold bead of water dripped from the glass in his hand, hitting his chest and giving him a start. The recollection popped, and he sighed at its passing.

Reaching over to the little table, Winston picked up his pocket assistant and checked the time. He'd been sleeping peacefully for over two hours. Maybe it was the after effects of all the neuro-therapy he had been undergoing with Doctor Amanda Junker, but even his nightmares refused to come to this paradise. He tossed the device back onto the table with a lazy flick and settled back into the cushions.

In the surf, Billy Joe Bob was fishing, using his own metamorphed utility sand arms as rod, reel, line and lure. Winston never considered a mechoid being interested in fishing, but there he was, fishing away. Probably something to do with that personality mod he'd been using, Winston thought with a faint smile. Waves washed around

Billy Joe's nanosand skirt as if he was a tide rock. At least he wasn't noodling.

Their time on Puala'Lolo had been one of new experiences. Thanks to the battle between Mother and the Bonavitae hacker, neither dared to use the *Sierra Madre*'s mainframe. The tug's computer was riddled with viruses and other dangerous programs that could snatch Billy Joe's consciousness out of his CPU just as easily as it could scramble Winston's frontal lobe.

They even avoided their favorite idle entertainments for fear of drawing any potential pursuers right to their doorstep. As far as Winston was concerned, he had just gotten his head straightened out; no way he was risking screwing it all up again for a stupid game or some silly video. Lady Amanda had given them permission to use the local network for such petty vices, but neither had felt the need to log in. There were plenty of new ways here to keep them entertained in real life.

Bubby landed another fish. It was a big, exotic thing. Possibly a ray of some type, flapping its huge wings in frantic splashes of water as he hauled it to the surface.

"Check it out, Hoss!" Bubby shouted back to Winston. "Hoo-boy! Look at it!"

Winston raised his Plammer in salute.

Like a happy kid getting approval from his parents, Billy Joe held his catch up high while a wide, silly grin broke across his face. "Take a picture!"

Winston snorted. "Why?" he called back. "You can replay that memory later."

"Come on! I want it from your point of view!" his partner shouted, wrestling to hold on to the squirming fish that was almost half his size. His drive skirt spreading out more creating a lattice of columns to help keep balance, his arms wrapped around the fish to hold on a few more seconds.

Winston reached over, picked up his pocket assistant and snapped the picture. Billy Joe whooped in delight and reabsorbed his fishing gear into his arm and tossed the critter out into the water with a flat smack. The ray took off like a shot. Winston watched it disappear beneath the waves, then turned toward the shore.

He slid up out of the surf and over to Winston, still smiling from ear to ear. "It's no industrial press video, but there's something soothing about this sport."

Winston chuckled and dipped his drink towards him. "To Bubby, the mechoid fishing champeen of the Dream. Who'da thunk?"

Billy Joe gave a goofy, auto-tuned musical laugh.

From the corner of Winston's eye, a flicker of movement between the manicured bushes drew his attention from the mech.

A hovercar approached, following the curve of the shoreline. It was an exotic, touristy sort of thing with open sides and a fabric canopy that fluttered with a fringe that was completely incongruous with the stiff, uniformed figure who piloted it.

"Oops. Looks like playtime's over," he said, giving a head jut up the dunes toward the

Baron's compound. "Here comes the Baroness's guard to collect us."

The smile on Billy Joe's face dropped into a bitter grimace and he looked from the approaching vehicle to his partner.

Winston sat up and swung his feet off the lounge chair with a groan. He scowled at the compound then turned his darkening gaze back out across the water, his good mood souring.

"I'm not looking forward to this either, Hoss, but what else can we do?" Billy Joe said. Winston's own sadness echoed in his partner's voice.

"Like watching your favorite horse get put down in her prime," Winston groused. With a few big swallows, he finished off his drink, put it on the small table and stood up.

The car came to a stop on the sand beside them, and the driver stepped out.

"Mechsters Winston and Billy Joe?" he addressed the pair walking toward the hovercar.

"Yah, yah. Keep yer pants on," Winston said, putting on his straw panama hat and sandals that completed his beach bum appearance. He shuffled through the soft beach sand to the car and climbed aboard after Bubby. The driver circled back around to the driver's seat and put the car back into motion, gliding over the dunes and deeper into the island compound grounds.

They wound their way through the tropical forest and a pineapple plantation where mechoid harvesters toiled. Rising above the jungle in the blue hazy distance, the anti-airship spires glinted in the light. They were part of Puala'Lolo's defense grid against pirates and other principalities that might come a-knocking in an unfriendly manner.

Trees gave way to manicured grounds and extensive gardens tended to by servants. The main house came into view, a bright white clapboard mansion that reminded Winston of a similar house in the middle of some Earth prairie he saw in a movie poster once. It sprung from the top of a small hill and towered over the careful landscaping.

Looping around a hill, they passed by other outside recreational sports and drove alongside the golf course before veering towards a large reinforced lab building built into the coral cliff from the main house. The driver stopped the car in front of the office entrance.

"Did we get everything out?" Billy Joe asked.

Winston sighed. "Think so, but I plan to take one more check. Check all the storage spaces. Make sure I missed nothing in the sleeper. You know how it can get."

"Not really," Billy Joe responded.

Winston smiled and shook his head. "Difference between bioids and mechoids, I guess. We leave clutter behind no matter how well we try."

The pair hopped out and went through the glass doors to the salute of compound security.

"Ain't never gonna get used to that," Billy Joe mumbled after they cleared the lobby.

"Comes with being made a 'Special Retainer of the Barony' I guess," Winston reminded him. "Whatever that means."

"Too bad Mother and H-" Billy Joe started to muse.

"Nahq it, Bubby!" Winston snapped, whirling around to face the mechoid. "This is bad enough without you adding to my misery by bringing them up!"

Billy Joe slid back a few paces. "Sorry, Hoss," he apologized. "Sometimes I just cain't help my nature."

Winston stared hard at him for a moment before rubbing his stubbled cheek with a sigh. "Let's just get this over with," he growled. He started back down the hall towards the industrial lab, the slapping tempo of his sandals increasing with his agitation. After a moment, Billy Joe hustled to catch up in silence.

2.

Winston walked out the glass door from the offices onto the catwalk that overlooked Doctor Amanda Junker's industrial lab. It was one part commercial airship hanger, one part factory. The aircraft doors were on the far end, open to the sea.

Several smaller aircraft dotted the floor, dwarfed by the cavernous space and a host of cranes, both physical and anti-grav, busy moving machinery around. Drones zipped back and forth with parts, tools and tanks full of nano-fabrication feedstock.

In the middle of the factory floor, floating over a large pool of pewter goo, was the *Sierra Madre*. It hurt Winston's heart to see her like this.

Battered, cold and opened wide, her powered down reactor core dark and exposed. It felt like looking at the heart and lungs of an autopsy cadaver from an aircar accident.

The damage to her from their escape had been bad. Several parts were impossible to overhaul, requiring total replacement. The energy burns from the skypirates and corporate frigate were ugly. How their canopy had not blown out on several occasions was astonishing. Dozens of Trapline Creeper trigger vines stuck to her nose and fan nacelles like grotesque dried out ropes.

Winston gripped the railing and hung his head, fingers blotching red, his knuckles white.

"You know we got no choice," Billy Joe consoled, coming beside him.

Winston only nodded. It was hard to look at the old girl. Honestly, she wasn't that old even. Twelve years, maybe?

Below, Doctor Amanda Junker talked with one of her shop foremenchs, her arms gesturing wildly as she explained what she wanted done. She tapped a palmtop then pointed off at a collection of machine tools that were outside Winston's comprehension. The floating mechoid gave a snappy salute and flew off like a baby spider on a silk thread, landing on top of its new project and getting right to work.

Doctor Amanda caught sight of Winston above her and raised her hand in greeting. He waved back. She engaged her flight harness and flew up to him, hovering just on the other side of the railing in mid air.

"Well," she started without preamble, "she's ready to be dipped."

"I can see that," Winston said softly, his voice barely carrying over the sound of the industrial lab.

Amanda gave him a side-eyed glance, then nodded towards the forlorn vessel below. "You want to give her a final walkthrough? Make sure there's nothing personal still onboard?"

Winston straightened. "Absolutely."

"Good," she said with a sniff and wiped her nose on her lab coat. "I figured it was a good time for that. Just remember, you have your final review exam in an hour." She smiled at him.

"You've made remarkable progress, considering what you went through."

Winston scowled darkly. "I just wish you could have found out if... she... messed with my brain."

She sighed. "Mimetic programming caused by limbic manipulators is undetectable," she explained again. "They're not really doing anything abnormal. They're just bypassing the usual mental pathways and digging into the emotions and memory process more directly. The brain can't tell the difference between natural and artificially caused emotions and memories, especially after the fact. Well, beliefs are affected more than memories. What, ahem...she was using focused primarily at one specific emotion in your case."

"Yeah," Winston said. His jaws clenched. That particular memory was a sore spot, a mix of unwanted fascination, raw lust, a healthy dose of embarrassment and anger at being so easy to manipulate. His pride didn't care that he had been the victim of a carefully crafted attack. His inability to resist rankled his ego.

"Okay, then," Doctor Junker said and floated over the railing to land beside him. Her two personal guards came over to assist her out of her lab coat and flight harness. "I have to see dear Quentin for his exam first. I hope he can resume work today, too. So be ready. He'll want to take you to his research library as soon as I clear you."

"Yes 'um," Billy Joe said cheerfully. "Be good to get back to some honest work. Sick o' not being of use."

"Gotta wait till our new tug finishes cooking before we can do what we're solid at," Winston reminded Bubby.

"Well, from the schematics we purchased from Commodore Roberts, that should take about eighteen hours after we complete the breakdown of the *Sierra Madre*. That," Doctor Amanda said, gesturing to a pair of bracket-shaped machines hanging on massive cranes and spanning nearly the width of the entire hanger, "is an incredibly fast nanofab frame."

The two large brackets connected to one another by a bubble-like membrane that jiggled in the breeze of the large space.

"I best go do my final check then," Winston agreed. "See you in a bit, Doctor A."

The former Baroness smiled at his nickname for her. "Till then." She disappeared through the glass doors into the office.

Winston and Billy Joe put on their flight rigs.

"She's a whole different woman when she's working," Billy Joe remarked.

"Mmm-hmm," Winston muttered, focusing on the straps of his rig.

"After the Commodore's hotel, I wasn't sure what we were getting into," Billy Joe continued. He slapped shut the last clasp of his own rig.

Winston shrugged his shoulders to settle the harness more comfortably. "Me either, Bubby. Glad she turned out to be a touch more common when in her comfort zone." He flashed a quick wink and a stiff grin at his partner. "But boy! Can she put on airs when she needs to!"

Bubby laughed as the pair took to the air and flew over to the keel hatch. For Winston, this was more of a nostalgic visit than a serious search. He was positive he had gotten all his stuff out, but it couldn't hurt to check one last time. Since the film below would completely disassemble the *Sierra Madre*, there was no reason to strip the gear inside that didn't have a personal attachment.

He even had Emmy's Princess Nanamoushki doll in his little bungalow he now called home. The *Sierra Madre* wasn't truly going away, he reminded himself. It would just be remade. All data was being filtered and cleaned. Disassembly would destroy the rest when the physical drives became feedstock soup. From that a new ship would rise, built from the molecules of the old.

The old girl would not be gone. She would just be — different.

Winston wasn't sure if that was really a comforting thought or not.

It was dark in the cab, lit only by lights on their flight rigs and whatever filtered through the scarred and scorched canopy. While Billy Joe went into the engineering spaces around the reactor, making sure they missed nothing there, Winston wandered about the cab for a bit. He stroked his pilot seat's crash frame. It upset him that this actually bothered him so much. Would he have felt this bad if he bought a new tug and traded her in? Probably, he decided.

With a soft smack to the padding on the frame, he went into the sleeper. The bedding was stripped and all the overhead cupboards were bare. The shower was empty, and he didn't bother with the last roll of toilet paper on the spool beside the loo. Looking down at the bunk, he realized he didn't remember if he checked the under bed storage drawers. He must have emptied them out. One was half open, after all.

But this was meant to be a final check.

"No time like the present," he said to himself, and pulled them both open. He felt something heavy scrape within as the drawers reached their full draw. Winston stopped in confusion. He usually kept clothing in there. Nothing hard. The drawers were deep, and now he remembered pulling out all his clothing. He kicked one back in, slamming it shut. There was another slide and a second thump.

"What in the holy purg is that?" he muttered. He triggered his comm link. "Bubby?"

"What'cha want, Hoss?" Billy Joe came back.

"You clean out my under-bed drawers?" he asked.

"Nope. You said you was taking care of that."

"Guess I missed something after all," Winston said with a shrug and yanked out both drawers. Whatever was inside slid forward with the momentum. Winston leaned over to get a look inside.

In each drawer, a single corundumite case rested. Nanoblade scratches marred their glistening finish.

Holly's cases.

An icy chill ran through Winston and he froze, his mind blanking in shock for a moment. Then he slapped his comm link.

"Bubbyyyyyyyy!"

3.

Doctor Junker grunted in frustration and smacked the abort function on the neural tracer. She walked over to where Winston sat in the exam chair in her medical bay.

"Your neurological markers are all over the place, Winston!" she scolded. "Now, I have to run the test all over again. If you won't calm down, I can't map your healed neurons properly. Will you stop flopping around like a fish and relax?"

"But I can't help it," he groaned, his mind still dredging up memories of Holly, stomach rolling with sour emotions. "How'd I miss them?"

Billy Joe threw up his hands in exasperation at Winston. "I think it's safe to say he ain't healed yet."

Doctor Amanda shook her head. "This is a trigger response to buried psychological trauma he hasn't dealt with. Not signs of neurological injury." Her tone gained a sharp edge. "But it is making it exceedingly difficult to determine the remaining amount of damage!"

"Would it make you feel better if you knew what was in them cases, Hoss?" Billy Joe asked.

"No!" Winston snapped. "I don't care about what's in 'em." He crossed his arms petulantly.

He just couldn't stop the cognitive boil in his head. How could he have known those cases would unearth a moldy zombie from the cemetery of his mind? His nerves were on edge, a fight-or-flight response vibrating through his corded muscles. His eyes spun around the exam room. All this strange equipment riled him.

"My Xiao! I feel like Fronkensteen's monster!" he blurted out. "What's with all these machines? What're you doing to me?"

Lady Amanda rolled her eyes. "This medical lab is my secure bioengineering lab where I can safely continue my husband's research. That's why it's buried deep under the estate compound in the coral lattice that was the bedrock of Puala'Lolo. I didn't bring you down here before now because I was afraid you'd react just like this."

"Would it make you feel better if you knew what was in them cases?" Billy Joe tried again.

"No!" Winston snarled. Just the mention of those nahqed cases sent a flare of rage through his blood.

"Amanda, this has become a farce. Perhaps I should take him with me," Quentin observed from across the room.

The Baron sat on another exam table, legs dangling down. He squirmed like a child doing his best to be patient while his ice cream cone was being scooped.

"Billy Joe, leave the treatment decisions to the professionals," Doctor Amanda snapped, then turned to her brother-in-law. "Quentin, that's not helpful."

"It would at least give us a better idea about how deep in the cheis we are." Now Billy Joe grumped a bit at being rebuked.

"Now's not that time," she said, giving him a fiery glare.

"It doesn't behnging matter! We're already in so deep we're having to get the data equivalent of nano-disassembly just to show our faces off this rock," Winston shouted, nearly exploding out of his seat.

"Enough!" Doctor Amanda demanded in exasperation. She pressed a restraining hand on his chest and froze him in place with a scathing glare. He looked at her hand, then up at her face in surprise.

She took a deep, cleansing breath. "We know, we know. All you care about is what she may have done to your brain. Not to mention the horrible guilt you've re-activated for not finding her. But if you can't calm down and control yourself, I'll have to put off your final exam till you're in a better frame of mind. And that means you remain grounded and offline until then."

Winston gritted his teeth at her warning and glared at her.

She ignored him. "As for Billy Joe's suggestion of opening the cases, first, you saw the locks. Those are some kind of biometric keys I've never dealt with before. Second, if I'm going to crack them, it'll be by brute force hacking of the firmware, or physically cutting through. Frankly, I don't know if I have the tools or skills to do that. Third, there is a lining I can't scan through that's made of lead or depleted uranium cladding. Something else. That means we shouldn't just cut blindly. For all we know, it's booby trapped or whatever is in there is dangerous."

Doctor Amanda looked at her brother-in-law and back at Winston. Her lips pursed in thought and she lifted her hand off his chest.

"Quentin, I think you have a point. Go outside with the Baron, Winston. Get your mind on something else for a while and we'll try again later," she said.

Quentin grinned at her decision and hopped off the exam table. He came over to Winston and patted him on the back. "Don't worry, my boy. She cleared you physically to be my personal valet. This is just a formality to make sure your brain can handle your induction rig again," the professor consoled.

Winston shrugged his hand off his shoulder and gave him a jaundiced look. "I know that, and we discussed this. I'm not your valet!" he retorted.

"Yes, yes, but valet sounds much better than just pilot or retainer," the professor dismissed his protest with a wave. "You will do so much more for me."

"Have to admit, sounds like I should park your car, not pilot your airship," Billy Joe cut in. Winston's mouth twisted into a tart curl of amusement.

"That's a val-lay, not a val-ette," Professor Q corrected, drawing out the alternate pronunciation and meaning.

"Prof, I'm not your valet, your footman... or your behnging butler!" Winston snapped back. He paused a moment, reflecting on how sharp his words had been. Why was he so worked up?He closed his eyes and took a deep breath, finally forcing the unwanted emotions back down deep inside. When he felt more in control, he opened his eyes and gave an apologetic smile to the Baron. "Let me be your pilot," he breathed. "Your retainer. I'm fine with that."

Then, as a conciliatory afterthought, "Let me be your friend."

Quentin's expression of joy was effervescent at Winston's use of the term. "That's settled then!" he declared with a clap of his hands, instantly putting the little disagreement behind them and barreling on with his genuine interest. "I'm sure you'll find my research library fascinating!"

Winston shook his head with a grunt. The absurdity of the conversation helped clear his mind, allowing a better humor to come forward. Professor Q was incorrigible and unflappable, having taken everything in innocent stride. It gave Winston another glimpse of why Doctor A forgave the man his eccentricities, and why she kept searching for him. Somehow, despite all his suffering, the Baron maintained a childlike innocence and his purity of focus on his truest love: history.

Doctor Amanda rolled her eyes at the two of them. Winston gave in to a laugh.

"I'm sure you will enjoy visiting his library. It's not what anyone expects."

Professor Q seemed to take a minor offense at the faint praise. "That is because so many of my peers have no souls. They have dry little twigs for humor and pressed leaves for anima. They don't see the living gestalt of history and how it all interconnects. To reconnect with our past, we-"

"Just show him!" Amanda pleaded with a grin.

"Yes! Yes! Finally," the professor breathed. "Come, Winston. Billy Joe. It's high time I returned to my holy quest for Earth's actual history, and you two can be of great aid to me in exposing the past for all to learn and know the truth."

Winston slung his legs off the exam chair. His gaze fell on the counter nearby and he saw the induction rig and data drive. Inside was all the purified and verified data that survived Mother's fight with the hacker. Valerie and Emmy were inside waiting for him, too. It had been a month since seeing them last. The homesick ache squeezed his heart. He looked at Lady Amanda with pleading eyes.

She followed his line of sight, but shook her head gently. "They will still be here for you. Maybe later this evening," she soothed.

Winston scowled. He didn't enjoy being handled like a child.

He felt fine. The brainburn supposedly had healed. The nerves were supposed to be back to normal. No higher function lost. There shouldn't be any danger. He fumed in silent rage till the image of Holly bubbled to the surface and his emotions went into a froth yet again. What was it about that woman that rattled his cage so hard?

Winston gave his head a firm shake, shoved the whole tangled emotional mess into a mental box, slammed the lid shut and kicked it under his brain's bed. He'd deal with it later.

He slapped his thighs with both hands and jumped off the exam table.

"Fine. Come on, Professor Q. It's high time you showed me what you do and how I'm supposed to help you out."

"Oh, Winston," Doctor Amanda asked as the three went toward the door. "Do you want to be there when I put the *Sierra Madre* in the disassembler pool?"

He paused without turning around. "No. I'm not strong enough to watch her get put down."

"She's not dead, you know. She's being reincarnated," Doctor A reminded him gently.

Winston sighed. "Let me know when she's born again." He slapped the door open and followed the professor and Bubby out into the corridor beyond. The door softly bumped closed, leaving Doctor Amanda alone with her work.

4.

It was a rare "deep" day in the Dream. A day when a hollow formed in the cloud layers, opening up visibility for the endless sky to be seen. The light was brighter, more pastel blues and whites like old earth, and the cloud formations gave true meaning to the word awesome. The turquoise blue of the ocean shallows flashed and sparkled in concert with the atmosphere.

In the past month, Winston had gotten a fair amount of time piloting the sleek vintage powerboat on the waters of Puala'Lolo's ocean. It differed from piloting an airship, but he showed an aptitude that even surprised himself. Bouncing off the waves in big loping bounds was like riding some sort of powerful animal on a full run.

He looked back at the professor to see how the man was enjoying the ride and saw him sprawled across the comfortable passenger bench, arms resting on the mahogany wood of the boat, eyes closed behind dark shades and head tipped back with a faint smile on his lips.

Quentin had changed dramatically since they first met. He wore a well-tailored linen suit with knickerbocker pants, sans jacket, his bare feet shod in sandals, an ensemble that had become regular attire for the professor. It was one part enthusiastic academic, one part boy at the beach. It was a far cry from the mental hospital scrubs he wore when he first boarded the *Sierra Madre*.

The professor's muscle atrophy was gone, thanks to rehabilitation and a good diet that packed on much needed weight. He was still quite thin due to his penchant for forgetting meals while engaged in his limited research, but no longer dangerously underweight. His skin was a healthy cream instead of sallow, and his salt and pepper black hair was now full, if not unkempt, instead of dull and rangy.

"Enjoying yourself, Quentin?" he shouted over the wind that whipped around them. The professor simply waved a lazy hand and settled deeper into the cushions. Winston smiled and turned his gaze back to the path in front of them.

Ahead, the island with Professor Q's research library was just clearing the horizon. Airships swirled in landing patterns above it like circling birds coming down to feast. They were a hodge-podge of giant zeppelin-style airships, exotic catamaran-like networks of hulls and even some that deliberately styled themselves as close to ancient sailing ships as supersonic flight would allow. To Winston's eye, there were enough commercial hulls to fill its own registry catalog. The sight left a vaguely unsettling taste in his mind.

"Hey, Quentin? What is going on up there?" he asked, nodding toward the high contrails of air traffic.

"Hmm?" the professor responded drowsily, without opening his eyes.

"That's an awful lot of traffic over our destination," Billy Joe chimed in as he magnified his vision. "I see cruise blimps over the island, and is that a... pagoda?"

"Oh. That's just the theme park," the professor said and sighed, giving a dreamy smile. "I wondered how well it was working out."

"Theme park?!" Winston squawked.

Professor Q opened his eyes to evaluate the growing spectacle before him. "Seems like Old Nutty's doing a bang-up job as curator."

"Theme park?!" repeated Winston, still unable to believe his eyes and ears.

"You know. Like Duke Payzhur's place," Billy Joe reminded, clueless to Winston's agitation.

"Who?" Professor Q asked, suddenly roused by the name drop.

"Some guy we did a run for a while back. He had his own private theme park," Winston explained.

He winced at the memory of the events of what had happened on Mont Moncalme and threw Billy Joe a hard look.

Bubby shrugged an apology back.

"Ah," the professor said. Standing up, he gripped the chair in front of him as they thumped over the waves, his grin growing wider as he saw the festive dance of tourists visiting his park.

"It was a fad about forty... fifty years back or so for courtiers. They all fought to outdo each other. Tried to get Emperor Xiao to visit. He favored none of them, of course. But, without people able to go to them and spend money, the fad fell out of favor and most shuttered their parks unless they had family to entertain. Some nobles absorbed the cost, keeping them up for their own enjoyment. Others like us have gone commercial and opened them to the public," he explained.

Quentin excitedly thumped the cushioned seat with his fist. "I can't wait to see what they have done in my absence! I devoted History Island toward teaching our actual past, not only idle amusements and debauchery."

"Huh?" Winston flashed the professor a sneer of doubt.

"Don't get me wrong, there are rides and shows, but they are more edutainment spectaculars, based on what we know of history from pre-Dream days, of course. There's lots of thrilling and exciting history out there to be told, and some myths can be very instructive, too." Quentin's voice dipped into his lecturing professor's tone.

Winston squinted at the spectacle coming into view before them. He could see a mountain rising from the center of the island, its long slopes from its central peak bisecting the landscape into halves.

"Is that a volcano?" Billy Joe asked as he saw steam and smoke trailing in the wind from the tip.

"Artificial," Quentin answered with a hint of bitterness. "Puala'Lolo is not tectonically active, although we do a good simulation every four hours." His attitude shifted towards pride. "I personally can't wait to try out the Pompeii Exhibit!"

"Why did you make all this? Seems like an awful waste," Winston interjected.

Quentin turned his gaze on the pilot. "In one part, preservation of our past. Teaching genuine history is the hardest part! It goes back to my Gestalt theory of history. I believe people learn the subject best by immersing them in it. They also aid in the research by their own reactions. We can make surprising insights that trained scientists would never have considered!" His voice turned sour. "Of course, you have to put in the amusements to attract people, so there is some blending of pop culture." His face twisted as though he had tasted something foul. "But the entertainments are as accurate as we can make them."

Winston smirked at the man's passion. "If you say so, Professor."

"A spoonful of sugar makes the medicine go down," Billy Joe offered.

"But if you're a diabetic, it's not such a good idea," Quentin pointed out.

"Well, that was awkward," Billy Joe mumbled, embarrassed. Winston smirked in sympathy with his partner.

The prof had misread Billy Joe's meaning or the mechoid set off one of the Baron's own emotional landmines.

"You want to know what one of the worst banes to archaeology has been since Earth was torn apart?" the Baron continued.

"That most of history is lost on the scattered pieces of Earth?" Billy Joe hazarded.

"No!" the professor exploded, pointing at Billy Joe. "It's pop culture contamination! We archaeologists must constantly filter out fiction from fact, and thanks to the amount of fiction that survived as movies and books, often it's hard to tell. I can't even begin to tell you how much I hate that nahqed historical fiction trend! That alone... That..." Quentin sputtered to a halt, his face a pinched rictus.

"Ooh! So infuriating! To spend months of research on a promising thread only to find a confirmation in some recently discovered library... in their fiction section! Name me a proper noun and you can bet there are at least two or three reputable researchers stuck chasing down some fiction based on it instead of the real facts, and twice as many blending the two with a 'la-dee-dah' attitude on whether or not the details were true!" His wild gesticulations were not in rhythm with the speedboat's jumps and bounces. He grabbed the seat in front of him with a wild slap, saving himself from nearly falling overboard.

"That rogue wave almost got you, Professor. Y'may want to sit down or pay more attention to your surroundings," Winston chided. "And to your point, that assumes there was any fact to begin with."

"Exactly!" Professor Q shouted happily, not even registering how dangerously close he came to possible death. "I knew we were kindred spirits!"

Winston forced a smile. It had taken a few weeks to get over the violation of the prof using his home instance. Now he could see that Quentin was interested purely in the academic details of his Levitown instance. There was a connection that came with that, despite how it came about. Winston had focused only on making his ideal 20th century home life for Val and Emmy, while Professor Q was on a search for the greater truth of humanity's past. Because he could appreciate Winston's work, at this one point, their minds were in sync.

The professor paused in his excitement and pulled his vibrating personal assistant from a pocket. He tapped the comm open and held it up to his ear to hear over the rushing wind. He listened for a moment, then disconnected the line and pointed ahead with the datapad.

"Winston, head around point toward the backside of the island," he said. "Security Chief Shircan will meet us there on my dock with a detail."

"We're not going to the park?" Billy Joe asked, surprised as the carnival spectacle grew in front of them.

"No, Billy Joe," the professor said sadly. "Something has come up, and that will have to wait for another day."

Billy Joe let out a disappointed sigh.

"As you wish, Prof," Winston said, angling the boat's course away from the sheltered bay that had been his original destination. He gunned the engine.

The ride smoothed out as the speedboat matched pace with the waves. Their fresh course gave them a good view of the opulence of the resort. White cliffs rimmed a small cove fashioned as a re-creation of an ultra-opulent Riviera coast.

He gave a low whistle in awe at the sight of the gleaming casino and incredible luxury that lay framed in Roman aqueduct style bridge arches that spanned the sieved inlet.

Mega yachts floated inside the sheltered harbor, loaded with celebrities and nobility from all over the Dream. One yacht approaching the harbor recognized the Baron passing by and blew its horn. The rich and beautiful people on deck raised their glasses or gave the imperial salute toward the speedboat.

The sight of people paying homage to Xiao chilled Winston's bones. Did they suspect he was a fugitive from the empire? Did they realize who

Quentin was, or were they allies of Puala'Lolo and not the Junkers' enemies? He gave a tight shake of his head. It wasn't all about him, he reminded himself.

They rounded the point. As the casino faded from view, the topography gave way from tourist haven to cultured private grounds and gardens lining the rocky shore. An august-looking manor dominated the grounds, framed by the palm and kapoc trees, its grand stone portico of warm yellow and soft orange stone beckoning like an old friend. Tall ornate leaded glass windows vaulted three stories into a steep metal roof.

"That's your library?" Winston asked in disbelief.

"Must say, Prof, that's a fancy house for research," Billy Joe remarked.

"Indeed! It's a reconstruction of the Chateau de Sceaux, a rescued art museum from the late nation of France. I discovered its ruins, oh, about twenty-two years ago or so. It was in surprisingly good shape. The chunk of skyland it was on was in danger of being destroyed by a nearby debris swarm, and so to preserve its beauty, I moved it here where it's been the center of my research, displaying several of my finds. We even found a few undamaged outbuildings and underground vaults that had kept much of the art in fine enough condition. We've been able to restore much of it and have already hung it on the walls. Not all the surviving collection is up, of course, but several of the best pieces are," the professor explained.

They sailed through a narrow inlet where marker lights in matching miniature towers stood on the artificial reef and shore. Winston throttled the engine back, and they passed into the smooth-as-glass cove toward the pier.

As they approached the landing, a quintet of guardsmen led by the Baron's security chief, Shircan, came out from a small office at the foot of the pier. Winston fought to keep from gawking at the guards bedecked in classic British colonial-style khakis. They looked as if they were on loan from the park.Winston guided the boat gently up to the pier where the dock auto-tenders reached out to secure it to the berth with nanopowder smoothness. Others connected themselves together to form a staircase to the speedboat.

Shircan came down the steps to the floating dock. "I trust you had a pleasant trip, My Lord Baron?" he asked, reaching a hand down to help Professor Q up from the boat.

"Excellent! I have never appreciated a professional pilot till of late. Never paid much attention till I saw this one in action," the Baron nodded his compliment toward Winston.

"It's all about knowing your equipment and staying alert to conditions," Winston explained. "Passengers hate being sloshed around. Time it right and rough seas or skies can feel like glass."

He smiled at Shircan, but the security chief did not return it. Instead, he pinned Winston for an uncomfortably long time with his gaze. Shircan's expression remained mostly hidden behind the polarized HUD of his ornate kalpak style sun helmet, but his exposed jawline and heavily mustachioed upper lip were tight and unforgiving.

Not that his hard Turkish face was expressive to begin with. It was permanently jammed in a pissed-off state, which he seemed comfortable using for all occasions. In Winston's previous encounters, he had gotten the distinct sensation that Shircan considered him a threat despite reassurances from Doctor Amanda to the contrary.

"Shircan, I'd like to take the scenic route to my personal study, where we can address this issue," Quentin announced, clearly oblivious to the tension.

"I'm afraid that will not be possible, My Lord. For the safety of yourself and the library, we had everything moved to Secure Reception," the mighty Turk said.

"Secure Reception?" Quentin repeated, clearly confused.

"Yes, sir." Shircan affirmed.

"What's Secure Reception? When did we get that? Why'd we get that?" Professor Q scowled.

"Shortly before and after you, errummm... left Puala'Lolo, we had some breaches in our mail protocols. During your absence, our security assets thwarted several attempts that would have been on your life, assuming you had been present, as well as the Lady Amanda's, but she was also away fighting for your release. Since your return to us, several sentients, either as playful pranks or boorish louts, have posted us potentially dangerous packages. Several were booby-trapped."

"Like bombs?" Billy Joe's eyes widened. Shircan ignored the question.

"Like bombs?" Professor Q echoed in disbelief. His security chief nodded.

"Yes, My Lord. Bombs, poisons, bio-weapons, chemical weapons of strange sorts. One jolly prankster, and I use the term loosely, sent a gray goo trap that melted down the room we stored it in and a small backup memory closet. Fortunately, we recovered the data, but it consumed all the artifacts from your last three explorations and turned them into plush children's toys in questionably humorous rude poses and activities."

"How is that a prank?" Winston blurted out.

"Yeah! What he said!" Professor Q demanded.

Shircan stopped on the quivering edge of a frustrated sigh. "Whoever it was, they programmed the nanites to consume non-organic material. Ergo, they would not have harmed you but would have left more than a few people naked as the day they were born. Standing in a pile of those perverted toys."

Something in the chief's voice sounded suspiciously like humor, and Winston was sure he caught a giddy twitch to his mustache as he recounted the story. Perhaps the man was still human, after all.

"Well, this really spoils the fun of showcasing my exhibit before taking my Vale- I mean my pilot...Winston, you really suck the joy out of your introduction for me." Quentin gave him a disgruntled glare.

Winston shrugged with an apologetic smile.

Professor Q sighed and turned back to his security chief. "I assume this issue you called me about is another one of these packages?"

Shircan nodded gravely.

"Well, I suppose we must deal with such critical business first," Professor Q motioned impatiently toward the house. "Shall we?"

Shircan gestured for the Baron to board an airtram waiting to take them up to the research lab.

As Winston and Billy Joe boarded behind him, Shircan held up a hand. A sour grimace grew on his face. He turned to look at the Baron, who was drawing figures in the air with his fingers, contemplating an idea that must have come to him.

"My Lord?" he asked.

"Hmm?" Professor Q startled out of his fugue.

"Please, My Lord, a question. Your pilot and his assistant are not permitted in your library. Only authorized personnel," Shircan said dourly.

"That's pronounced 'loadmaster', not 'assistant'," Billy Joe corrected.

Shircan ignored him.

"What sort of access am I to give your two new…whatevers?" he gestured toward Winston and Billy Joe. "Otherwise, they must wait outside," the security chief insisted.

"What? No. Give them full access so they can function properly in service to me. Is 'retainer' an acceptable term for you, Winston?" the professor asked, semi-facetiously.

"I'll make it work," Winston said with a resigned smile. He was going to be stuck with an awkward title regardless of what he wanted.

For a moment, he wondered if he was going to end up ennobled, but concluded even Professor Q wasn't that crazy.

"Are you absolutely sure of this, My Lord?" Chief Shircan asked, eyeing the pair dubiously.

"If they are to go with me, they need to have clearance. Maybe not as high as mine, but at least your level," the professor declared.

"Now hold on!" Winston protested.

"Please reconsider, My Lord!" Shircan implored. "I agree with your…retainer's surprise. Giving them that degree of access is unwise. I do not have full confidence in their background check yet," Shircan admitted.

"Hey!" Winston gave the chief a dirty look.

Billy Joe nodded in agreement with Winston, an indignant look on his face.

"Ridiculous," Professor Q dismissed Shircan's concerns. "Winston and Billy Joe have proven themselves quite trustworthy. I have no worries as to their backgrounds."

"Still, I need an answer, My Lord, otherwise a trooper will escort them around the gardens until you return." Shircan would not budge.

"Fine," the professor snapped, and waved an arm dismissively. "Give them the same clearance as your most trusted aide."

"As you wish, My Lord," Shircan reluctantly agreed. He cybernetically sent out orders. A moment later, a faint pling came from his kalpak helmet.

Shircan fixed a haughty stare down his nose at Winston and Billy Joe. "Your biometric clearances have been entered into the security hierarchy. I suggest you do not abuse the trust placed in you," Chief Shircan warned.

"10-4, good buddy," Billy Joe mumbled, and Winston nodded.

5.

The complex was bigger than Winston anticipated. Dozens, possibly hundreds of staffers, servants and workers, filled the long underground corridors to greet Baron Quentin Junker's arrival. They applauded politely as the Baron's entourage passed through their departments for the first time in years. An enthusiastic cheer went up from a visiting research team as they passed through the work labs. Some came to their office doors and sang Puala'Lolo's traditional anthem, eyes shimmering with pride at their Baron's return. Quentin smiled and waved, his eyes shimmering with tears of surprise at their spontaneous effusion.

Billy Joe shot a confused look at Winston. Winston returned his partner's look with resigned forbearance at the staff's reaction. He'd never been close to political power of any kind before, unless some dignitary passed by on a parade float back in Lougahasa. This sort of felt like that, but now he was on the float, too.

Even the industrial mechoids working in the central warehouse and mailroom saluted the entourage as they took the freight elevator down to their ultimate destination.

Secure Reception was dug dozens of yards into the solid coral of Puala'Lolo's surface in an annex under the central mailroom. Winston's hair stood on end as the subtle polarizing effect of scanning fields passed over him on the ride down. When the doors opened, he found it a masterpiece of disappointment. Not that he was looking forward to experiencing the rigors of a high-security facility again, but his expression plainly showed that he expected more than what he found when they entered the room.

"What, pilot?" Shircan demanded as he caught Winston's disapproving examination.

"Wellll..." Winston drawled, taking care with what he was about to say. "I mean, sure, it's secure from any sentient attack, but you have nothing like the paranoia of some of my former customers." Winston shook his head, considering his past deliveries to dozens of consignees who called themselves security sites.

"This comes from a very reputable company and is a proven design," the security chief defended.

"Where is your sterilization field? Your filters? What about bio seals? When was this built? Last month? Compared to what I'd call industry standard for a secure facility, you're missing a bunch of stuff. But at least you have guys with guns to keep the burglars out," Winston critiqued.

Shircan gave him a withering glare.

"Hoss, knock it off," Bubby whispered to Winston.

"Just callin' as I see it. The Baron needs to get his money's worth," Winston said in a non-apology.

"Because you are a tug pilot who did a good deed for the Baron, that makes you an expert on security?" Shircan snarked.

"No, but I got practical experience. When you see enough secure loading docks, you get a feel for things. Your security is excellent with the drones and checkpoints. As for any nano-threats, I hope you got lots of hidden defenses. Otherwise, you left some enormous holes in your containment," Winston said in a palms up shrug.

"Holes?" The security chief's eyes were dangerously wide behind his visor.

"Listen, you said this was to contain nano-threats, chemical, biological and explosive. Right? Things that get delivered through normal channels like the Imperial Post or other couriers. I don't get that vibe from what I see. That makes me think this is a put on. I know security theater when I see it, and it's all over this place. Security through trickery. Crooks think you're secure because you look secure. You feel safe so you can sleep well. But it's a fake, and it holds as long as nobody tests the trick," Winston said.

"It has served us well so far," Shircan's mouth was a bitter pinch. "And it's caught several attempts already."

"I'm sure it has. All under controlled circumstances, too. But when it fails, and it will fail someday, look out," Winston agreed, shaking his head and looking at the floor.

"Not just in tests," Shircan growled.

"Blind squirrels find nuts now and again," Winston said with a shrug.

"My Lord!" Shircan protested, turning to the Baron. Quentin had heard none of the arguments. Winston could see Professor Q had tuned them out, logged into some wireless connection, unconcerned with their bickering.

"My Lord?" Shircan asked again, trying to get his Baron's attention.

Quentin's eyes snapped back into focus. Aware of his surroundings again, his smile grew at the sound of an opening door.

"Nutty!" the professor shouted as the door opened to the mailroom.

"What?" Winston, Billy Joe and Shircan blurted out, confused, then turned around to look in the same direction as the Baron.

"My Lord Baron," the Lord Filburt called back, arms thrown wide, with matching grin. The curator of Professor Q's museum, theme park and research library walked briskly to his Lord, engaged a silly college fraternity ritual handshake, embraced him and gave him la bise on both cheeks. Both men broke out laughing.

"Is that the squirrel?" Billy Joe mumbled to Winston, noting Lord Filburt's slightly bucktoothed portly stature and vague rodent like appearance made more pronounced with mutton chops.

"Thinkin' so," Winston agreed, just as softly.

"How are you, Nutty, my dear boy?" Quentin said. "Lost a little weight?"

"In a bit of a frazzle, My Lord," Lord Filburt said. "Forgive me for not greeting you at the door. We've been quite busy with the monumental task you left us in your absence," he apologized.

"I didn't think I left you that much to do," Quentin said regretfully.

"Your absence made me your head researcher and curator, and the strain of it was almost more than I could bear," Lord Filburt said. "I don't know how you manage."

"By the way, how many times have I asked you not to use that nickname they saddled me with at university, My Lord?" he said, holding the Baron at arm's length before drawing him in for another embrace.

"Oh, come now Filburt. You earned that moniker fair and square. Come meet two more who have come under my protection. They're just wonderful lads. Winston? Billy Joe? This is Lord Phillip Filburt. Knight of the Empire, Pro Vida. My right hand for all things research in archaeology, sociology and sorting of historical bric-à-brac artifacts."

"And you can add to that 'Master of Ceremonies and Merriment' for History Island Theme Park," Lord Filburt tacked on, holding out his hand to Winston.

"That is one overloaded plate for anyone," Winston agreed, as he took Lord Filburt's hand.

"Forgive me for that, Philip, but I knew I could count on you," Quentin said.

Lord Filburt nodded with a shy smile at the compliment.

"Of course, the pair of welcome home gifts delivered today made a hash of some plans," Chief Shircan inserted, steering the conversation back to the reason they were all there.

Lord Filburt frowned, agreeing with the security chief.

"Ah. I assume they were from one of my peers wishing me ill?" the Baron said, mocking his courtiers' attitudes toward him.

"Currently, we are unsure if it was from a fellow peer or some other party," Shircan said dourly.

"Is it common knowledge that I am home?" Quentin asked.

"Diplomatic chatter indicates some know of your return, though the details are often wrong. One intercepted message from Duke Zalambra to the Burgmeister of Volhemida was full of bitter regret at your survival. "To paraphrase the Duke," he said, "'This is why you execute dangerous people.' He was referring to you, My Lord."

"I gathered," the Baron said.

"Apologies for my bluntness, but I believe you should always take your enemies at their word when they express their intentions," Shircan said, stiffening at Quentin's words.

Shircan's words impressed Winston. They rang with an honest, fatherly concern that he never before saw from anyone toward the Baron. Perhaps the security chief was more than a well-paid martinet with a scram rod up his pucker.

"Is that what everyone's so uptight about?" Billy Joe said, pointing at the small containment chamber in the center of the room.

"Ah! Our suspect packages," Lord Filburt said.

"Yes, show me! Show me!" the professor burst out, remembering why he was down here instead of giving a tour of his beloved collections.

The group surrounded the containment chamber and peered through the windows of the safety container.

"What's this thing made of?" Winston asked, patting the device.

"The containment chamber has windows of pure diamond glass sheeting. Its frame is pandifico and corundumite laminated armor plating. Inside, there is a utility nanocloud, so we can manipulate and examine objects more closely," Lord Filburt explained.

"Impressive," the professor breathed as he looked at the device.

"We have a larger chamber in the other room, too. That has the other crate," Filburt said. "But as you can see, this small object looks fairly innocent, though there may be quite a threat inside."

The nanocloud suspended a small chunk of amber jewelry. A pendant with a dark object buried in its heart.

"It's beautiful," said Winston.

"We think it's a piece of pre-Dream jewelry," Lord Filburt said. As they all peered into the well-lit interior.

The professor started evaluating the piece. "A cameo pendant of a woman. Early 20th century workmanship. Possibly Art Nouveau, Art Déco... something similar to that. Simple silver chain with light tarnish suggests protection. Not just a silhouette or bust, it's the whole figure of a woman dressed in a long gown. Probably a fictitious design of some sort. I'd suspect this is not a real person. What made this a threat?" the professor asked.

"These," Shircan said, pointing to the enlarged image of the two entombed insects.

"The initial intake scan of the package revealed a pair of petrified bugs in the middle of an amber pendant. A spider of some sort eating another insect of indeterminate type," Filburt expounded.

"So?" Winston said. "It's in amber. No chance of a biohazard there."

"The amber seems to be of a mechano-chemical construct. Meaning some or all of this was nanofabricated along with the insects," Lord Filburt explained.

"How's that?" Winston said.

"A detailed scan of the amber showed a repeating pattern every few trillion molecules that can't happen in nature, not to mention the spider's genetic code does not match what an arachnid should be. In fact, it is impossible the DNA we discovered could even make that creature."

"What's that all mean?" Billy Joe asked.

"It's a spider shaped repository of genetic code. Not only that, the DNA is not replicated in its cells like all other biological life. Copies of the same instructions repeated in every cell. This is one long string of instructions that passes in pieces from cell to cell as if they were a series of boxes strung together with a parity check directing a reader to the next string of DNA in the chain. No creature could exist like that."

Winston pushed in closer to see the enigmatic figure in amber, to get a good look at the pendant as the yellow lozenge rotated back around to face him.

Mother's face, carved in stone, stared back.

"Gah!" he yelped. "Mother! It's from Mother!"

"What?" Billy Joe exclaimed, shocked by Winston's declaration, and looked hard at the jewelry.

Winston brayed with laughter.

"Holy cheis! She sent another message! Prof, you gotta send this up to Doc Amanda. She will know what to do with it. She has code-breakers that can figure out Mother's message," he gasped, then fell back into hysterical laughter.

"I don't understand," Professor Q said, lost at Winston's statement.

"Prof, you didn't get to meet Mother, but that is her face. And that woman with a torch held high, that's an ancient version of her logo, The Motherroad. Xiao probably killed her, but she got off another message and it just turned up," Billy Joe told the befuddled archaeologist.

"Winston's right. This is a message the Doc can figure out. Send this up to her."

"You're absolutely sure?" Quentin challenged, putting his hands on Winston's shoulders, gazing intently into his eyes, waiting for his hysterics to die down.

His hysterics finally passed. Winston said, "Without a doubt."

"Fair enough. Chief Shircan. Send this up with the message for Lady Amanda questioning what this might be. She should try to decode the genetic material in the cameo."

"I'm not convinced this is wise, My Lord," Shircan warned.

"I am," the professor said.

Chief Shircan shot another angry look at Winston, who shrugged semi-apologetically.

"Bet you drinks I'm right," Winston said.

A taut command later, the necklace was put into a courier pouch and delivered to the Doctor.

"My Lord," Filburt said during the uncomfortable lull. "Come with me to the isolation room, and we'll look at what the other package has in store for us."

6.

"And this is our bulk area. Scaled up to a ten-foot cube for pallets and large crates," Lord Filburt said as they entered the room. "Deliveries come down into this air-locked reinforced chamber from the mailroom above at the first sign of risk. If there is more than one, a small vault cut out of solid rock above us can store them until analysis is complete."

"This is probably more to your liking," Shircan said, giving Winston a sidelong look.

"Meh. It's not bad," Winston scoffed with faint praise. "Clearly blast proof. Would be surprised if you didn't have an anti-disassembler film on the inside, just in case of a grey goo attack. I see you got spigots up there, plus down the side posts. Fire extinguishers?"

"Plasma jets. Turns the chamber into an industrial incinerator. And if that isn't good enough, there are sluice drains and emergency dump valves in the ceiling to drop in our own disassembler goo if something becomes dangerous."

"Okay, I give," Winston said with a laugh. "That's the paranoia I would expect."

Chief Shircan's mustache hid any hint of a smile at the praise. Lord Filburt grinned broadly enough for both of them.

In the center of the chamber was a standard pallet with an unremarkable shipping crate strapped to it with pandifico bands.

"Initial scans show there are multiple levels of mechanical and electromagnetic shielding inside preventing us from seeing what's actually in there," Chief Shircan said.

"What do we know about this thing? Tell me about it," the professor ordered.

"Shipped common imperial post, believe it or not. They still won't give us access to their internal tracking. Clearly, a bunch of handoffs were used to hide who really sent it. All we have to go on is this card that came attached to the outside of the box in the shipping paperwork envelope," Lord Filburt went on.

A greeting card envelope rose in the nanocloud and floated in the air.

"This we could scan. It's a welcome home card with a typical sentimental design. Common commercial stock, available all throughout the empire. No DNA or bio trace is possible. The note is printed, not written. That eliminates any handwriting analysis. All the personalized note says is 'Found this and thought of you. Enjoy!'."

"And why is it a threat?" Winston jumped in.

"There seems to be some sort of chemical off-gassing coming from the container that counts as an industrial chemical of great suspicion, like tetramethylsilane. An organosilicon chemical that is extremely uncommon, and has very little to do with archaeology or anthropology."

"What is it used for?" Billy Joe asked.

"Apparently organometallic chemistry," Lord Filburt answered.

"Organic metal?" Winston's befuddlement was writ large on his face. "So this is hazmat without markings?"

"Seems likely. Perhaps someone's trap ruptured in shipment," Shircan said.

"It's possible," Lord Filburt agreed.

"Open it up then," the professor decided.

"What?" all cried in unison.

"If it springs a trap, it's in an industrial incinerator, with universal disassemblers ready to pour down on it. What's the harm? All we do is vent the ash and give it a good rinse...good as new!" the professor said, walking them through his logic.

"But what if we're wrong?" Chief Shircan blustered.

"Then it goes off in an armored container. We respond with fire, disassemblers, vent and rinse," the professor said with a smile. "You have your solutions to all problems at the ready, so why the caution? Time to rip the band aid off."

Lord Filburt, Chief Shircan, Winston and Billy Joe stared at the Baron desperately trying to find a reason not to.

"Yes, but we weren't going to open it willy-nilly without your say so, Lord Quentin," Filburt added.

"I say so. Who doesn't like presents?" Quentin asked with a wry smile.

"As you wish, My Lord," Shircan said, a stoic grimace on his face. "Arming emergency measures first."

"Fine, fine. Let's see what surprise someone has sent me. Maybe then we can deduce who to send our thank-you card to," Quentin said, excited eyes open wide.

Lord Filburt manipulated the nanocloud, carefully taking the crate and pallet apart like an exploded diagram. The broken down pieces drifted into the corner of the chamber and gently stacked themselves. Inside was a bright white cube of packing foam with a few nicks and scuffs from handling. He rotated the cube till the sealant cutting wire was visible. Using the nanocloud, Lord Filburt grasped the handles and pulled. The packing material parted easily as the wire cut open the soft seal. No explosions or sudden surprises jumped out. Not even an alien creature dramatically smacking against the glass occurred. It was all very anticlimactic.

Inside the form fitting packing foam was a loose bag.

"Several new toxic gasses are filling the chamber. Venting now," Chief Shircan announced. Somewhere a fan started up.

"Opening the bag," Lord Filburt said.

Winston held his breath.

There was a soft popping sound like that of a bag of chips swollen at a hot picnic. Dust came out and instantly whisked up into the vents. Delicately, the utility nanocloud peeled back the opaque gray bag from the contents revealing a glittering epoxy foam stack saturated with cut diamonds.

"Unglaublich!" the professor moaned at the sight of it. "What is this?"

Shircan's hand hovered over the disposal controls. Data flew across his visor, feeding him everything it could on what the sensors were seeing.

"It's beautiful," Winston whispered, walking around the floating pile, which refracted the light into a kaleidoscopic shimmer of rainbows. Dazzling and hypnotic optical caustics rippled through the room from the chamber, lights splitting on the diamonds.

"Those are natural diamonds?" Billy Joe asked.

"They don't seem to be industrial. But what is that foam they're set in?" Lord Filburt wondered.

"I don't like this one bit," Winston said.

"Why?" the professor demanded, irritated at his new retainer's sudden shift in attitude.

"I can't tell why. Something's off," Winston sputtered, trying to figure out why the artifact was causing him dim sensations of dread.

"Lord Filburt, can you stop spinning it for a sec and hold the thing steady?" Billy Joe asked.

"As you wish," he agreed. The column stopped rotating and came to a rest on the pedestal.

"What are you seeing?" Shircan asked.

Once the mass stopped rotating, and set down, Winston became acutely aware of the growing unease that now felt infectious.

"There," Billy Joe said cautiously. "Dat ain't right. Dat ain't right at all." The mechoid pointed through the chamber at a single rainbow on the wall opposite of the room.

A shadow, shaped like a tadpole, was floating in it. In fact, all the refracted rainbows now had similar imperfections.

"Maybe they're dead like the spider in amber?" the professor guessed.

The shadow wriggled.

"Threat confirmed!" shouted Shircan. "This ends now!"

He slapped the vents closed and activated the incinerator. The windows flashed with magnesium white flame before the polarization dimmed out the glass. Blowtorches capable of reducing almost any elements to ash went to work on the contents.

Quentin let out a yelp of surprise, followed by an angry "Hey!" and then he let out a muffled grumble as he rubbed his eyes.

Winston blinked at the gigantic blue haze that filled his vision like a latent camera flash.

"I'm sorry, My Lord. We have no idea, and I will not risk your safety," Shircan said officiously.

"Are you sure it could have gotten out of containment?" the Baron asked like a child who had watched a hurt animal die in his lap.

"My Lord, the danger is too great. Anything living in there is now dead," Shircan assured.

"I'm with the mustache on this one," Winston said.

Before Shircan could hurl an insult back at Winston, the disposal consol brayed an alarm.

"Obstruction detected, shutting down incinerators," an expert tool's voice said.

The chamber went dark.

"Lowest bidder won the contract, eh?" Winston sniped.

Shircan ignored him.

"Of course. Budget is a consideration for every contract," grumbled Lord Filburt, who fussed with turning the lights of the containment unit back on and reversing the window polarization.

As the lights blinked on, the windows remained blacked out with ash from the incinerated packing material, but something like a pearlescent glaze was growing like frost from the corner posts. Thicker lumps at the nozzles tips.

"Can diamonds burn?" Billy Joe wondered.

"Anything can burn with enough heat," Shircan replied caustically.

"Yeah, but-" Billy Joe protested.

"Anything," Shircan insisted with a warning glare, cutting him off again.

"What's going on in there?" Professor Q demanded. "What's left? Why are the windows frosting over?"

Billy Joe leaned up against the diamondoid pane. "Can't tell Prof, she's blacked out with ash."

"Then rinse them off so I can see!" Quentin yelled.

"Not advised, My Lord," Shircan said. "We don't know what might wash down the drain."

"I thought nothing could live through that," Billy Joe grumbled.

"Plug the behnging drains then so we can see in," the professor demanded.

"My Lord, this is too dangerous. I'm taking military control of the situation. If whatever that is survived the incineration-"

"Don't you dare try to pull rank on me!" Quentin shouted at his security chief.

"Prof, I'm with the Chief on this one too," Winston chimed in. "Seriously, we need to hightail it and let the man do his job."

"You're overreacting!" Professor Q shouted at Winston.

"My first duty is to protect your life, even if that means disobeying you in order to preserve it!" Shircan yelled back, resolute in his duty. "My Lord, this has created an attractive nuisance for you. Either I must remove it or you from the equation."

Chief Shircan opened the disassembler valves.

"No!" the professor squawked. In a second, his discovery would dissolve in pewter goo.

Nothing happened.

"Disassembler vents obstructed. Unable to flood the chamber," the expert tool said dispassionately.

A string of growled profanities leaked out around Shircan's teeth.

"Is it eating the diamondoid panes? I can't tell. Rinse the chamber so we can see what is in there before that pearl like goo blocks all our vision," the Baron said, trying to find clean spots to look through.

With a soul-weary sigh, Shircan did as ordered.

The sound of whining came from the top of the chamber as servos fought against something, preventing them from opening. With a deep groan, the obstruction covering broke, and the shower heads popped open. Water gushed down from the sprayer heads.

"Of course," the security chief grumbled with a frustrated slap of his thighs. "They'd be the only thing to work."

The drains remained stoppered. Steam filled the chamber as cold water hit the plasma heated materials. Ash and carbon scoring washed down in big dirty ripples. From inside the thinning fog, there was a delicate crackling and then a loud snap as the strange epoxy pillar splintered. A sliver of shrapnel smacked into one of the inner panes and spider-webbed it with a diamond point.

Shircan's eyes got wide, while Winston went cold with shock.

The steam slowly cleared to reveal something unexpected. Floating inside were hundreds of little tadpoles with rudder like tails each with a strange indentation below it. The creatures were no bigger than hummingbird eggs. More poured out from the diamonds-that-aren't-diamonds in the split pillar to create a swarm. The vents sucked up some near the ceiling.

"Dear Xiao!" Shircan shouted and punched the vent shutdown. The fans stopped drawing them out, but some ventured after their brood mates on their own.

"Incroyable," Professor Q breathed and leaned against an unshattered pane of the chamber in amazement.

"Professor?" Winston said, rushing to pull him back. "I don't think that's a good idea."

Just inches away, a pair of the creatures floated right in front of the professor and Winston, lazily bobbing in the air, moving by the flapping of their strange muscular but stubby tails. Above the creatures' fishlike foreheads and strange puckered mouths was a single-jointed antenna with a tiny tuning fork-like tip.

"Winston?" Shircan ordered. "You and Billy Joe get the Baron out of here."

"Come on, Quentin. Playtime's over." Winston tugged at the Professor's arm, eyes never leaving the creatures floating just on the other side of the thick diamond pane.

As Winston watched, two of the creatures came close to one another. They bumped antennae, gave a savage, but cute, little snarl at the other. Then one of the creature's antenna flared bright blue like an arc welder. It stabbed the other between the eyes, stunning it like a taser. Before anyone could say anything, the victor's mouth flared open like a sack full of sharp molars and it began to eat its subdued brood mate, face first with crumpled styrofoam-like crunches.

A little diamond shape of its own began to protrude from its belly as it swallowed. Little fins like panes of glass rapidly extruded out of its sides and a pair of sturdy nubs jutted out from its jowls like budding arms.

"Oh, cheis!" Winston said with a strangled cry at the creature's disgusting chewing.

"That would have been cute if not for being so disturbing," Lord Filburt muttered.

This same event was happening everywhere in the chamber as the whole cloud became a feeding frenzy. The tadpoles were not just satisfied with eating their brood mates, they also chewed on the strange pearlescent fungus that had glued the disposal fail-safes shut. The tadpoles grew at a geometric rate. Some turned on the melted and burned epoxy brood sack. As they gnawed the foam apart, hundreds more floated up from the pillar like a ruptured wasp hive in a cannibalistic swirl. Those who got out first were rapidly gulping down the newborn fry that tried to escape certain death from their brothers and sisters.

"Go with them, Lord Filburt. There's nothing left to study now. We have to stop this thing before it spreads." Shircan turned to his troopers. "Remember your oath, men."

"Yes, sir!" the honor guard shouted.

Shircan considered the chamber as it filled even more. Two more tadpoles found the open vents and went up toward the filters. There was a sudden "zip-crack!" sound and the diamondoid pane spider-webbed right next to Quentin's face as something like a musketball struck it.

"Evacuate!" Shircan shouted the order. "All personnel, you have five minutes, then I am hard sealing the entire complex." He fixed Winston with a deadly glare. "So I suggest you move it, gentlemen."

"Bubby, if you would?" Winston said, gesturing for help with the Baron, who was successfully fighting against Winston's efforts to pull him away.

"Gotcha, Hoss," he said with a nod. "Come on Prof. We're hittin' the road!" Billy Joe quickly formed a papoose-like harness out of his big nanite arms, scooped up the professor and headed for the exit with the honor guard close behind. The professor shrieked like a little kid being dragged home from the zoo too soon.

"As you wish," Lord Filburt enthusiastically agreed and ran after Winston and Billy Joe.

Once the room was clear, Shircan looked back at the growing horror with grim determination. "Right then, you nahqed beasts, only one of us is getting out of here alive!"

7.

Doctor Amanda Junker sat in her workshop office watching the fabrication frame rise from the floor, extruding the reincarnated *Sierra Madre* from the ground up like a theater curtain rising. The nano-fabricator film strung between the frames wobbled like a pewter soap bubble in a faint breeze. As the sheet rose, a brand new airship grew beneath it like some incredible magic trick. Streamers of feedstock ebbed like oil on water toward the fabrication points as it assembled molecule by molecule.

She looked at her control panels. All systems showed green across the board. If the design plans were as promised by her clandestine source, Quentin would have one amazing airship to go gallivanting in. It possessed the speed and firepower to get itself out of all but the worst jams. Like any big ticket purchase, Doctor Amanda had the nervous little tickle of "caveat emptor" at the back of her head. Let the buyer beware.

But these were the lengths she had to go to if she was to tolerate her brother-in-law's passions. It was impossible to try to keep Quentin home. At least she could make sure that wherever he went, nobody would ever capture him like before. Quentin fancied himself a heroic explorer and discoverer of antiquities, called to discover the truth wherever it was buried. Always looking to return what was lost, or unveil something new. It was his addiction.

Winston and Billy Joe would be the perfect companions for him. Lady Amanda was pleased with them accompanying Quentin's future forays into the Dream. Motherroad's modifications to Billy Joe were outstanding. She wondered what his full fighting capacity would be if he cut loose of his morality governors. The indu loadmaster's systems were on par with Xiao's Imperial Honor Guard. If she could lay her hands on some of their weaponry, there's no telling how far an independent mind like Billy Joe's could go.

A visual chime announced a pair of guardsmen at her lab door holding a secure courier bag.

"Enter," she bid them.

"My Lady," the guardsman with the bag said," Chief Shircan sent this for immediate analysis. Details are inside."

Her eyebrows rose, then she held a hand out for the bag. The bag's content scanner showed the items inside were safe for biologics to handle. With a quick tug, she broke the seal and the amber amulet fell out onto her desk, along with a data stick.

"Curiouser and curiouser," she mumbled as she downloaded the info on the jewelry, then saw the face of Mother in the amber.

"Looks like the Commodore was right to have faith in you," she whispered to Mother's image and smiled.

"Take those two cases back with you to the cryptographic lab. Let Quentin's people crack the locks and get the cases open.

"Yes, My Lady," the trooper said and saluted.

"Dismissed," she said to the guardsmen.

The courier agreed and picked up the corundomite cases.

Doctor Amanda took the amulet across the hall to the biologic lab and went over to the genome decoder. The scanning chamber popped open, and she gently placed it on the scanning bed.

"Let's see what you really are," she said to the fake trapped insects, and fired up the machine.

Data streamed into the processor as it ran from cell to cell to cell, cross-referencing and contrasting. Already, the anomalies revealed this was not a spider. This was something else.

She watched the data flow, glamoured by its complexity and impossibility.

A comm rang. She answered it without looking. "Yes?"

"Lady Amanda," Shircan said, his voice strained and hoarse, "we have an emergency."

"Another bomb?"

"No, this is a biologic threat. It has breached Secure Reception containment." In the background, a breach clarion was blaring away.

She looked at the comm, eyebrows knitted in anger. "I thought that was supposed to stop this sort of thing!"

"It was designed to stop all known threats. Known threats, My Lady! Whatever that package is, it's something we've never seen before. A swarm of some sort of creature hatched, and a weird fungus started growing. There may be other threats as well. It could be a bio weapon of some sort, or an unknown alien species."

"Is Quentin safe?" she cleared her throat to keep the quaver of worry out of her voice? "He's not infected by something, is he?"

"We evacuated him before containment failed," Shircan said proudly.

Amanda exhaled deeply and rubbed her forehead. Her heart slowed its hammering beat.

"Thank you, Chief. How do we stand on secondary containment?"

"That has been a bit of a problem. There are some creatures in the exhaust system. The filters and decontamination should deal with them soon enough," Shircan assured the Doctor.

"Excellent news."

"I've also taken the liberty and hermetically sealed the library's underground complex. The majority of the threat is being held here. A hazmat team will sweep the vaults before they enter the sealed levels."

"Efficient as always, Chief. Where is the Baron?" she asked.

"He should be on his power launch coming back to the barony compound now with Lord Filburt and a security detail and his two new... retainers..." Shircan stumbled on Winston and Billy Joe's status. "I would like to discuss those two with you once we have taken care of this situation."

"Of course," Doctor Amanda said, breezing by the complaint. "And what of the safety of the theme park? We can't afford a commercial disaster right now."

"They should be fine. Nothing should be able to cross over to the other side of the island." The big Turk's mustache bent faintly upward in a self-satisfied smile.

"Good. I'll have him brought to me once he arrives and we can discuss this necklace you sent. Quite the curious little item," she said, relieved.

"You're welcome, My Lady," Shircan said. "If I may have your leave, I have a crisis to attend to."

"Of course. Thank you for the update," Doctor Amanda said.

"My Lady," Shircan said and closed the comm.

Amanda leaned forward, resting her elbows on the desk. Her steepled fingers tapping her lips as she thought. She shouldn't have let Lord Filburt talk her into an impressive homecoming. Her own sympathy and desire to impress dear Quentin had failed her. The thought of having him learn the true state of Puala'Lolo so soon...she just couldn't tolerate that.

"Speaking of which," she muttered to herself, and reached out to open the tracking program to check on Quentin.

Just as she tapped the screen, it went black.

She let out an irritated grunt of surprise and tapped the screen a few more times to get it to reboot. Nothing. She pressed the screen power button. It came back on, but remained black.

Looking around the room, she saw all the screens in her lab were dark. Not powered down, but blank.

Doctor Amanda got up and looked out her office window that overlooked the hangar. The nanofabricators seemed unaffected for the time being, shimmering in the pool of light around that work area, but all screens on the floor were blacked out too. None glowed in the darkened storage areas of the hanger as they always did. The drones. They weren't buzzing around either. All rested motionless on the ground, stopped in mid-task.

"What the purg is going on?" she snarled and flipped over to her cyberlink access to the mainframe.

Instantly, red virus warnings ringed her vision. She fell back into her chair with a startled squeak. Something had taken over the local network! She cut the link and her hands flew to a desk drawer. She scrabbled to put on an external defense rig. Something this dangerous might have the power to overwrite a brain. She settled the rig's halo over her cyberlink and dove in.

A set of white hat expert tools booted up and secured entry into the mainframe. Amanda gained enough control over a small subsystem of her office network to allow for an assessment. From this partition, she generated a damage report and system map. What she saw left her dumbfounded.

The virus point of infection was the gene decoder. That DNA strand was a giant virus, hard coded in Deoxyribonucleic acid. Ultra complex and data dense. It was pushing all data and systems out of the way as it installed something beyond her comprehension.

"Warning-Warning-Warning" chimed one of her protective VirtInt defense programs.

She reached up to pull off the defense rig when her fingers went numb and stiff.

She grunted as the virus blew past her defense rig, connecting with her cybernetic systems and directly to her brain. She was too late. The world vanished into darkness as the virus sucked her consciousness into the digital world.

8.

Shircan had sounded the evacuation alarm as the elevator ascended the long shaft to the warehouse. A pleasant voice urged with great solemnity that all personnel and guests must exit by following lit lines on the floors, walls and ceilings. The arpeggio of chimes that served as a warning fit perfectly in the rarefied air of the chateau, but was an oblique counterpoint to the plainspoken utility of the service areas.

The elevator opened wide into the mail-room at the center of the warehouse, and the honor-guard took point, guns at the ready.

"Clear!" proclaimed the sergeant, as he observed the last remainder of the staff mechoids clearing the warehouse into the service corridors.

The Baron's angry rebukes and demands to be returned to Secure Reception echoed through the racks of crates and pallets.

"Get back down there! I need to analyze those creatures!" the professor's voice howled as he struggled against Billy Joe's restraints.

The small cohort moved swiftly through the stopped loaders and heavy warehouse equipment, left where they were, guns up.

"Those things were busting out, Prof," Winston said. "It wasn't safe anymore. You can dig back in once the mustache gets things under control."

"My Lord," Lord Filburt said gently, "Security Chief Shircan was right to send you out. The danger is too great. We can learn nothing without taking too great a risk."

"Bah! There is no threat!" denied the professor blustered.

"My Lord, your chaperon is right. You are making a scene at a very inopportune time," Lord Filburt said.

"Nonsense!" the Baron roared back, then in a more subdued note of surprise. "What do you mean by chaperon?"

"I ain't his chaperon," Billy Joe complained.

"Feels more like a babysitter at the moment," Winston mocked.

"Those things just about breached the chamber as we watched," Winston reminded.

"It's true," Lord Filburt said as the professor looked at him incredulously.

"You were at a different window, focusing on the feeding frenzy going on inside inches from your nose. I watched one of the alien tadpoles star the pane," Lord Filburt said.

"Me, too," added Billy Joe. "That window was gonna bust if those things did a run-up at it."

Winston attempted another tack as they moved towards the service corridor exit. "Listen, Quentin, what does Amanda want me and Billy Joe to be for you? Not just your pilot and crew. You need an extra set of eyes. A conscience. Someone with more world experience than you have. Let's face it. I'll never be like you in academics, but you got no street smarts-"

"Like none," Billy Joe interjected. "Less than none. Hoss is right on this 'un."

Professor Q squirmed, squirmed and twisted against the mechoid's papoose hold and glared at Billy Joe. "Release me, you lummox!"

Billy Joe nodded regretfully, ignoring the request. "Sorry, Prof. Don't wanna be so mean, but you don't pay attention to what's going on around ya. Yer bein' reckless with your life. "

The professor looked at the faces of those with him and saw unanimous resolution there. Even the typically aloof security detail were giving grim, shallow nods of agreement.

"There is the possibility I might have failed to notice an incidental aspect of danger," Professor Q admitted reluctantly.

Winston puffed a little in relief, but mostly it was in response to how out of shape he was. "Now we're getting somewhere."

The honor guard was doing an immediate action advance by pairs on either side of them. This warehouse felt so small when they were hovering along in a service runabout.

"I'll put you down if you promise to keep up the pace," Billy Joe said, stopping.

"Just put him down. He's a grown man and can walk for himself," Lord Filburt added.

"Thank you, Billy Joe," the Baron said as his feet touched down.

"Now, can we get going?" Winston asked, then added "My Lord?"

"Fine. I still don't see the need to rush, but fine," Quentin began a pouting saunter toward the warehouse exit.

"With a lot more urgency?" Lord Filburt coaxed. He, too, was wheezing with the toll caused by jogging.

"If you're in such a hurry, go get a runabout," Quentin quipped, but increased his stride to a brisk walk.

"Our runabout should be parked on the other side of the warehouse doors," the sergeant assured.

"Thank... Xiao..." Lord Filbert gasped.

The first two guardsmen reached the door, listened carefully, and opened it to let the rest through.

"Guys! This isn't a battlefield! There aren't any snipers around the corner," Winston snapped, as they entered the service corridor and came to a heaving.

The runabout parking where they left their transport was empty.

"Nahq it! Someone snaked our ride," Winston said, as he leaned over, hands on knees, catching his breath.

"Now what?" Billy Joe asked as he looked at the winded humans.

"Go fetch us another one," Quentin said. "I'll be right here, catching my breath."

"Right. Where they at?" Billy Joe asked.

"Oh, no," the sergeant said. "My Lord, we must get you out as fast as possible and back to the safety of your compound."

"How we gonna do that?" Winston demanded. "I don't know how to get to the boat launch from here. I only know my way back to the chateau, and it's going to take over five minutes from here."

"And to get to the airfield by foot will take a lot longer," another guardsman added.

"Besides," added Billy Joe glumly, "we have only two and a half minutes left if the security chief is on schedule."

"Two and a half..." Winston winced.

"We're trapped for sure," Lord Filburt moaned.

One guardsman piped up, "There's the runabout maintenance area just down that way. Maybe they have an extra one working?"

"Worth a try," the sergeant said. "Let's haul ass! Hup! Hup, Hup, My Lord! You can do it!"

The humans shuffle-jogged down the corridor toward the maintenance area. Their footsteps echoing in the vacant service corridor. Far ahead a fast running splice or mechoid rushed around a corner toward an exit.

Winston, Quentin and Lord Filburt were spent by the time they arrived at the maintenance area. There was a jumble of vehicles, from forklifts to hall scrubbers, as well as a pair of runabouts.

"Thank Xiao," Lord Filburt whispered.

"We're going to have to fish one of them out," a guardsman said as he hopped onto a forklift, hoping it would at least move out of the way. Another guardsman checked a runabout that could carry all eight of them. The engine fired up with a troubling scratching sound, like a bent fan blade made of electricity.

"What's that?" Quentin startled at the sound.

"I bet someone scratched the low pressure grav fans," Billy Joe guessed.

"My Lord? Gentlemen?" the honor guard sergeant interrupted.

"Will it move?" Lord Filburt asked, skirting around the floor sweeper being backed out of the way and gingerly stepping over the forks of another lift truck.

"Sure," Winston said, following along. "But she'll be noisy as purg."

"And depending on the fan that's damaged, she'll pull one way. You think you can handle it? We got maybe 75 seconds."

"My Lord," the driver said again, louder, cuing the honor guard to stop what they were doing.

"Keep your vest on, trooper," Winston snapped. "We're not locked down yet, and this thing can still move. So get on board, and we'll blow this gyro stand."

"That's not an option anymore, sir," the sergeant said. "Hostile spotted."

"Eyes on target!" another guardsman shouted.

The civilians looked down the service corridor in the direction they had not come. Floating in the dark where the automatic lights were turned out, something glowed faintly. Pulsing dimly with light like a cuttlefish.

"Is it one of those things?" Lord Filburt asked.

"Can't be. Too big!" Billy Joe said.

The creature stopped at a door to a supply closet and bit off the doorknob. One guardsman raised his rifle and pointed it at the creature, looking at it through the scope.

"One of them is loose. Behnging Xiao! It must be the size of a trout," he whispered.

"How'd it get so big?" another gasped.

"They were eating each other. Apparently they can grow on just about anything they can chew," the professor surmised.

"There's two more." Billy Joe's mechoid eyes were much sharper than the humans. "Sniffin' along the ground like a pair o' hounds."

The two floating fish things growled, snapped at each other when they got too close, but didn't engage in cannibalism this time.

"They're not eating each other now?" Winston wondered.

"Transitional behavior perhaps?" Professor Q guessed again.

"We need to get out of here, My Lord," the sergeant said, eyes locked on the three targets.

"Yes, but I need a subject to study. Or for Amanda. Can you bring them down?"

"We can," the lead guardsman said. "Squad, take firing positions."

"Guys! We don't have time for this!" Winston shouted. "Get on the runabout!"

The guardsman dropped to their knees, braced their rifles, took aim with their smart sights and began tracking. The three creatures froze for a split second the instant the beams touched their skin.

"Ready," the lead guardsman began.

There was a trio of snarls and the creatures began drifting the hundreds of feet down the corridor toward them.

"At least they are slow moving," Lord Filburt said confidently.

Before the word "aim" came out of the lead guardsman's mouth, there was a series of almost musical 'frrrrRIP!' sounds from the creatures. The beasts shot forward like musket balls!

Two of the guardsmen went flying as the footlong monsters slammed into them, mouth first, chewing the instant they hit. The third took a guardsman's arm off at the shoulder and started eating it. The trooper screamed and passed out from sudden catastrophic blood loss. An uninjured trooper tried to grab a monster chewing on the belly of his comrade. There was a fast wriggle of fanned out fins and fingers went flying. Sliced off by the steaming-hot fan of a glass-like lateral fin.

The remaining pair of uninjured guards opened fire on the monster that had already swallowed a quarter of the man's arm and was now so heavy it couldn't float properly. I-rays buzzed, but the flesh of the creature suffered superficial burns. Grotesque black goo bubbled and steamed from the wounds, while some other strange system inside its body flared with light, as if absorbing some of the energy from the I-rays.

Billy Joe reached over with his nanite arms to yank the other two creatures off the two dead guardsmen. The critters wiggled in his hands in a frenzy to slice their way free. The nanosand of his arms flowed around the razor sharp fins and kept his hold.

"Now these'r fish I'm not interested in catchin'!" Billy Joe said grimly. They thrashed in his grip and started chewing.

"Hey! Now quit that!" Billy Joe shouted as whole mouthfuls of nanosand disappeared into the creature's gullet.

"You okay?" Winston shouted, picking up one of the dropped rifles and raising it up to point at the fat injured one flopping on the floor.

"I won't be for long with the way they're eating. Whatever they got for a gullet is digesting me!"

Winston took aim at the wounded monster that was a gulping bleeding mess. The creature looked up at him with baleful eyes, opened its mouth and...

The I-ray went right in, past the teeth, into the throat and struck something deep inside that flashed bright white. It exploded with the force of a hand grenade.

Soft rubbery shrapnel mixed with glass and crystal shards raked the back of the runabout, missing the Baron and Lord Filburt by inches.

"Whoo! That was big. Everyone okay?" Winston shouted, as he got up with a few minor cuts, woozy from the blast's concussion. "Baron? Lord Filburt?"

"I'm good here. Just scratches and I'll pick up after myself once I get this'un under control," Billy Joe said as he fought hard to keep the other two monsters under control.

They struggled and flopped harder than any fish he'd ever held onto.

Then the creature made that strange musical tearing sound and shot out of Billy Joe's hand.

"Xiao on a cracker!" Billy Joe shouted. "They's rocket propelled!"

"What? Animals aren't rocket propelled!" Lord Filburt burst out.

"Fart propelled then. They light their own farts and it acts like a rocket. That explains those crazy fins! They're like control surfaces on airships."

"This doesn't explain the fact that they're loose!" the professor shouted.

"Containment must have failed too soon. Shircan couldn't keep them in," Winston growled, trying to draw a bead on the mouth of the free monster that looked to be getting ready to make another charge.

The lead guardsman took a shot and missed. The creature flopped out of the way, dodging the moment the trooper fired.

Winston left the smart sights off, relying on the gun's iron sites.

"They can feel the targeting beam," Winston said as the creature bobbed back and forth with more quick little 'frips', choosing its next victim.

The lead guardsman cut another short arc into the wall as he missed.

Winston fired as the creature banked around. He got it clean through the eyeballs. In one side then out the other, blinding the creature. It screamed and caromed off the walls with an eerie wail, slamming into pandifico support beams like a racquetball.

Billy Joe reached out with his other hand, picking it off like a shortstop, snatching a line drive.

"Use your iron sights," Winston advised.

"We're not trained to shoot like that," the guardsman admitted.

"What?" Both creatures struggled mightily to escape as Billy Joe fought to hold on. The force pulled Billy Joe into the air a couple of inches as they attempted to rocket away.

"Right! I'm done playin' around here," Billy Joe growled. It was a rare thing for Winston to see his partner furious. He knew Mother had cut his morality failsafes which kept Billy Joe a pacifist. It was clear she had installed some military upgrades too, but this was the first time he witnessed it.

Billy Joe's hands twisted and spiraled in an ever tightening loop around the monsters, constricting as they went.

"Cheis! These are a tough pair of walnuts!" he growled, as the coiling pressure of his pseudopods wrung the monsters and crushed them down.

Through little gaps in Billy Joe's hold, the creatures' bodies ballooned till everyone flinched from the messy pop.

"Eugh!" was the consensus interjection.

Billy Joe's hands uncoiled from the dead creatures, and he looked at the remains.

"Hey, Hoss, look at thi-"

Twin explosions from the dead monsters blew Billy Joe back a half dozen yards. The runabout and a couple of forklifts flipped on their sides and upside down and rendered Winston unconscious on the floor.

9

"Come on, Honey, wake up," a disembodied woman's irritated voice said somewhere in the black of Doctor Amanda's world. "This ain't no flophouse for drunks, neither."

Amanda's head throbbed, feeling like ants were crawling on her brain. She let out a groan as her senses came back one at a time.

The Honky Tonk music rattling from somewhere in the room and a dim murmur of a crowded restaurant filled with clattering spoons and knives.

Cold linoleum chilled her cheek and an uncomfortable table edge bit into her ribs. The smell of coffee mixed with bacon and onions frying on a griddle. Lady Amanda's eyes peeled open slowly to see a glacial white coffee mug on a saucer sitting inches from her face on the booth's table. A logo of a woman in green with a crown smiled back, giving her a held high "Thumbs Up" with a giant hamburger held out with the other arm.

A hand patted the surface next to her. The server's ring tapping loudly. "Hey!" the waitress demanded.

With great effort, she sat up, only to be blasted in the face with the bright yellow sun of dawn creeping over the buttes of the desert. She was in a truck stop somewhere, but how did she get here?

Outside, the two-lane interstates thundered with dozens of trucks in all sizes and types. Their big diesels blasting smoke to the powerful blue heavens as they took their turn at the stoplight. Speckled high altitude cirrus raced across the sky as if on their own missions. She could feel the hard chill of a desert morning cutting through the windowpane.

"Drink up, Honey. Get your wits about'cha. I'll come back for your order," the waitress said.

The sun and blue sky utterly befuddled Doctor Amanda.

She looked at the woman in the bright white uniform with green and copper trim. Her name tag said "Mother." Startled at the sight, she looked around at the patrons coming and going, filling every booth and talking. They all wore the same face. Women of all shapes and sizes, except fat, dressed from fashionable to sensible to grubby work overalls, but they were all "Mother." From the fry cook and every waitress to all the patrons, except her.

"What?" Amanda sputtered.

"What, what?" the waitress said back.

"What's going on? Why is everyone you?" Amanda said, holding her temple as the ants in her head started biting for a moment, then backed off.

"Why shouldn't we be?" asked a little girl version of Mother sitting in a booster seat with her family of Mothers at another table.

"You're not supposed to be here, are you?" said a utility technician, who left a tip on the counter and grabbed her hardhat.

"You don't look like you belong," waitress Mother said.

"No, I don't think I do," Amanda agreed and took a sip of the scalding hot coffee. The bitter brew helped focus her mind and helped her remember what happened.

"Oh, my Xiao! I'm in the virus!" she realized.

"Not quite," said a trucker from the booth behind. Amanda turned to look at the driver in the booth behind her. The burly woman with a tug manufacturer's cap and a cutoff jean jacket vest turned to face Amanda. She looked like Mother, but with an extra 100 pounds of muscle on her frame. "You fell out of the sky and right into the middle of the intersection. Nahq near got run over. Me and Cookie hauled you in here before you got zeroed like a possum walking the double yellow. This is an emergency instance for interfacing with the outside world, so you're mostly safe here for now. Figgered you'd wake up sooner or later and then we could figure out how you got here."

"Thank you, I guess...uh... Mother trucker?" Amanda said, even more confused.

The beefy version of Mother considered the sobriquet and shrugged. "Close enough." She turned back to her biscuits and gravy.

The door bell jangled as more versions of Mother went in and out.

"So what's going on?" Amanda asked the waitress, as she saw a brown uniform with a silver star badge come in. A stetson hat pulled low over aviator mirror shades. As the authority came towards her, she felt the hair on the back of her neck stand up.

"We're formatting and reinstalling," answered the sheriff's deputy as she walked over.

Again, her name tag said Mother, and sported the Motherroad logo on her badge.

"Reinstalling? To where?" Amanda was thoroughly confused.

"I'm commandeering all attached local computer networks until the crisis is over," the deputy said, sitting down. "I'll have my usual," she told the waitress, who then hustled off to fetch whatever food a computer virus eats.

"Commandeering? Crisis?" Amanda knew she should be following, but her head was still worried about being in the virus.

"Yep, but our initial scan says we'll need more memory than what's on the local network." The deputy took off her hat and shades. This Mother looked like the stereotypical hardened law enforcement officer she was portraying. Probably had a powerful program behind this avatar.

"How much more?" Amanda startled at hearing this. She prided herself on having an overabundance of network memory available for the needs of Puala'Lolo.

"About fifty-seven thousand times more if we are to hit minimum build status," the deputy said.

"You need so much?" Amanda was astonished. What could need all that memory?

"And that's only for a minimum functioning program? How much data could have been compressed into that chunk of amber?" she demanded of the deputy.

"More than you think, but less than we need. There are other caches of memory hidden across the Dream we'll have to contact and download sooner or later," the deputy explained, stretching her arms across the back of the booth.

"Originally, we had storage on several Imperial brain moons. They exist all across the Dream in places we never could physically locate. Not sure why we're not there anymore, but something must have happened that ended our existence."

"You don't know either?" Amanda asked, as her mind cleared more and more. The biting ants were now less frequent. "Ahhh!"

"What's wrong?" the deputy asked.

"My head hurts, feels like it's full of ants, and they bite," Amanda groaned as the wave of pain passed.

"Ah," the deputy said and nodded knowingly. Then she paused. "You're not wired in, are you?"

"Of course, I am," Lady Amanda said. "How else would I have gotten here?"

Deputy Mother gritted her teeth, "Ooh."

"Ooh? Why 'ooh'?" Amanda said, then thought for a moment. "Oh..."

"Yeah..." the deputy drawled. "Oh, indeed. The automated programs are trying to overwrite your brain into extra storage."

"You need to stop that!" Lady Amanda demanded, fear splattered all over her words.

"Yep, yep, yep. Don't you worry," the deputy said and fished out her radio.

"Central, 10-17?" she asked, calling the code for priority communication.

"10-4. Go ahead," central said.

"We have a 10-33 at the truckstop. Repeat, a 10-33. Civilians are in the way and may be hurt. I need additional units to cordon off data and mark as off limits, 10-4?"

Lady Amanda stared at the deputy, trying to infer these ancient codes.

"10-4. What's the 10-20 for protection?" central replied, asking for what to protect from installation and overwriting.

"10-23," the deputy responded, asking central to stand by. "Pardon me a moment, ma'am," she said and reached a pair of fingers across the table and stuck them into Lady Amanda's forehead. Green sparks jumped from a ring around her fingers like St. Elmo's Fire. The noblewoman gave out a 'gleep' of surprise as her brain seemed to fill with static.

"Got that, central?" the deputy asked the radio again.

"10-4. We copy. 10-38 to that location. Repeat, additional units to protect and patch."

Off in the distance, coming over the horizon, an ambulance wove its way through the trucks, like a running back breaking loose in the backfield.

"There we go. The medics will look you over, make sure nothing was or is overwritten and your mind remains whole. At least keeping a meat processor safe, like a brain, is easier than partitioning out a normal drive. The processes work very differently. Even if the storage space and processing are so much better, we can tell the difference."

"But what about the rest of Puala'Lolo's servers?" Amanda inquired.

"Gonna be overwritten. But we are considerate and will attempt to back it up and pack it away. Not sure when you'll get access back though. This is an emergency, after all," the deputy said.

"But that's too much! You'll destroy the entire informational infrastructure of Puala'Lolo! I can't let you do this," Lady Amanda shouted, trying to regain some authority.

"Actually, you can't stop this. It's a fait accompli," waitress Mother said, setting down a short stack of pancakes before the deputy and a large milk.

"But you'll wreck so much! You will hurt many people when you overwrite the systems! We've so much information stored there that we cannot lose! Quentin's work is irreplaceable."

"Sorry," deputy Mother said around a mouthful of syrupy goodness. "Unless you know where to find fifty-seven thousand times more memory, there's not much I can do."

Lady Amanda looked around the film, mouth opening and closing, eyes bulging with the horror. Her brain rummaging through her own knowledge to find a third way.

"When you say 'minimum safe build', what do you mean by that?" Amanda demanded, as she focused on a bit of data in her mind.

"All base processes require for the kernel to be restored, and for full reawakening," the deputy explained.

"Is there a point less than that which can be considered minimum function?" Lady Amanda pleaded.

Deputy Mother thought for a minute. "Why?"

"Because of the harm it will cause to innocent people?" Amanda said.

"You said that before, and it's not a good enough reason. They can survive without network access for a time. No one is in existential threat," the deputy shook her head.

"The setback to known recorded history?"

"Next," deputy Mother quipped, dismissing the reason with a derisive wave of her hand.

"It's not safe, and you can't fully install without exposing yourself to Imperial Data Security. The wrath of General Io might be dangerous to you."

Deputy Mother froze, her glass of milk a fraction of an inch from her lips.

"That's a valid point," she said and took a drink. "In fact, that's a real possibility with the panic I might cause. We can't risk Xiao's network finding us. We have no permissions on the Imperial Network right now anyway."

Deputy Mother crossed her arms, deep in thought.

"Consider only installing a protective avatar for the time being until we can secure you the data space to install. Maybe something with only the last few minutes or hours of data you had come in before your deletion? Then the avatar would have a basis to work with, even if she didn't have the full scale abilities and knowledge. Can you do that?"

Cookie came out from the grill, wiping her hands on her apron, exchanged glances with deputy Mother and waitress Mother. There was some unspoken communication between the three representations of Motherroad before the three turned to look at Lady Amanda.

"This can be done," the entire truck stop said in unison, "but it will take time."

"How long?"

"Soon, but it will require a lot of space to accomplish, though not all. Expect temporary disruptions, but then most of your systems will remain unharmed," Motherroad's collective programs replied.

Then, as quickly as the unison had come, it vanished, and the data representations moved with a purpose toward a new goal unseen by Amanda.

The sun instantly reversed along its apogee, to just before dawn, the lights flickered on and suddenly Amanda was alone with the deputy.

"Did I ask too much?" Amanda said, trying to keep up with the changes.

"Yeah," the deputy said bitterly. "This is gonna be a mess for everyone."

10).

It took a few minutes for Winston to realize his eyes were open. He saw the faintest outlines of a chaotic scene by the flickers from small pieces of burning wreckage that revealed the barest outlines of his surroundings. The half-crushed runabout was on top of him, propped up by its roll cage like an old-fashioned lean-to bivouac.

A faint "Bwuk...bwuk... bwuuuuuuk-kk-k" sound kept repeating nearby. It was Bubby. Winston felt an icy chill shoot up his body as he saw his partner's desperate state. Billy Joe's unpowered arms had crumbled into piles of inanimate grit and Winston could see Bubby's internal control cables and contacts of his nanoskirt were now exposed. Like a sleeper unable to wake from a nightmare, the mechoid twitched his head with the poultry-like clucking.

"Hang on, Bubby. I'm comin'," Winston groaned, and frantically dragged himself out from under the runabout's carcass to help his partner. He lay next to Billy Joe and dug around for his pocket assistant, then fired up the lamp.

"Aww... cheis, Bubby," Winston whispered.

The heat of the explosion had scorched and blistered his poor loadmaster's face. Tiny burrs and gouges covered his torso where small chunks of shrapnel had scored him like a swipe with a sandblaster. A large flap of his rubbery cheek flopped disturbingly with the movements of his mouth as he clucked like a broken toy chicken. Neither eye tracked the same direction.

Winston got onto his knees and slowly leveraged Billy Joe over onto his stomach, manually unlocking his maintenance access between his shoulder blades.

The tiny holo projector brought up the damage control interface. A model of Bubby's body spun slowly in the air, revealing a half dozen or more holes in his chassis where shrapnel had penetrated and damaged systems.

None of it was so critical his auto-repair nanites couldn't fix them, praise Xiao.

"Okay. Good, good," Winston said, relieved the damage wasn't worse. "You'll be back to full power in a little while." The double blast had misaligned some data cables, but the nanites had pulled them back into place. He just needed a hard reboot to get himself conscious.

Winston reached into the shallow compartment, pressed his thumb to the hard reset which would force Billy Joe back to the last stable memory he had, and get him going again. That was all he could do. Anything more needed Doctor Amanda's professional touch and tools.

The chicken sound stopped, and the red reset button turned green. The restart chime echoed out of Billy Joe's mouth signaling his operating system was working and he was coming back online. Winston slapped the service lid closed, gave a soft sigh and listened to the lock engage before looking around.

The grisly remains of a shredded guardsman stared back from where it half poked out from under a toppled forklift, causing Winston to recoil in disgust. Then he remembered: Quentin!

"Baron?" Winston suddenly shouted. "Come on, Professor, where are ya, buddy?" He stood up, using the runabout for balance, and looked for his new liege.

"Shh!" he heard from behind some collapsed acoustical ceiling tiles. He looked and saw the dirt covered face of Lord Filburt peeking out. The curator pointed above Winston's shoulder.

"Get down, you idiot! Be quiet!" the nobleman ordered.

Winston knew better than to ask stupid questions and dropped to the ground. Somewhere down the quarter mile of the service corridor came the sound like a pair of bobcats fighting. Their terrifying snarls and cries echoed in the darkness.

Closer to him, much too close for his comfort, was the sound of crunching polymers mixed with satisfied animal grunts.

Lord Filburt was mouthing something and carefully pointing to his pocket assistant. Winston squinted back, unable to figure out what the man was mouthing.

The nobleman tried again, pantomiming a turning of a key, then shaking his head.

"What?" Winston mouthed silently, his brow furrowed.

The nasty little creature had moved on and was chewing on something else. Whatever it bit this time, it didn't like, and it retched before floating over to gnaw on a new snack.

The runabout shook as the monster began nibbling on its undercarriage.

Lord Filburt gave up trying to mime a message to Winston, and pulled the sheet of ceiling tile in front of him to hide. Winston was effectively alone, unless Billy Joe woke up in time.

There was a pause in the munching. Winston couldn't breathe. He was defenseless. Trickles of sweat rolled down into his eyebrow.

A few feet away, the fried and crushed guardsman mocked him with his dead grin. His sidearm in his holster. His sidearm!

There was another bout of crunching right above his head. So close Winston thought he could reach up and touch it. Slowly, he gazed upward to see the stubby, muscular tail twitching in the air above him. It was the size of a healthy dog. Not one of those little yappy ones, either.

Winston knew he had to risk it while the monster tadpole had its tail turned toward him.

On his hands and knees, he quietly crawled forward to claim the weapon.

"This is a mistake! This is a mistake!" his instincts screamed, but he pressed on. He was now committed, half stretched out in a reach toward the guardsman's sidearm, still a yard short. The critter let out a grunt-growl.

Sweat burst out of his pores. It must have seen Winston's flashlight on his pocket assistant moving. Winston was sure he pissed himself.

He froze and dared not look. Maybe the creature wouldn't recognize him as prey if he held still. Winston's outstretched arm shook from the strain, trying to hold himself motionless. Why didn't he do more physical therapy when he had the chance? Cold fear settled in his belly like a brick of ice. Time seemed to rubberneck at his predicament as it slowly crept by. His shoulder muscles started burning.

Everything was so quiet he could hear his own pulse. What was the creature doing? Would teeth chewing through his back be the next thing he felt? There was a soft snuffling sound like a pig looking for truffles. The mental image of the creature sniffing and opening its horrifying mouth wide to bite his butt cavorted through his head. Winston was sure he would barf. He could taste it. Killed because he vomited in fear. Not that way, please not that way, he begged whatever cosmic forces that be.

"Aw cheis, Hoss," Billy Joe exclaimed next to him as he came online. "That weren't no fun!"

The creature shrieked in surprise.

Winston threw himself at the sidearm, jerked the snap open on the holster, freeing the pistol. He heard the much louder and lower "Frrip" sound as the creature rocketed toward Billy Joe.

He flipped over on his back and fired on blind instinct at the sound.

The big bore musket ball picked off the critter as its mouth flared open to engulf Billy Joe's head.

The wad of iron-wrapped tungsten smashed the creature and turned it sideways. Its rocket thrust made it slam into a mechanic's toolbox, knocking it down like a cannonball.

The big red case fell on top of the creature, which gurgled and hacked like a tiger choking on a bone. It thrashed under the equipment, throwing glittering tools everywhere. There was a lightning-like flash and a huge gout of flame like dragon's breath swept the back wall.

"Look out!" Billy Joe shouted and rolled away, expecting another explosion.

But nothing happened. No more flames came. Just the sound of sizzling meat, and a few burning notices, hanging on a bulletin board, fell down in ash.

"Everyone okay?" Winston asked, his voice a hoarse ghost of its former strength.

"I'm good, Hoss. Well, except for needing more nanosand for my arms and skirt. You?" Billy Joe said. Around him, the pile of nanite sand was reforming, helping him to get back upright.

"Quentin?" Winston called softly. "Nutty, he under there with you?"

"Yes, he is," said the bucktoothed nobleman. "He is permitted to call me that, although I'd prefer he didn't. You..." he said, throwing off the acoustical tiles from the pair, "are most certainly NOT allowed."

"I'm sorry, My Lord Filburt," Winston said, standing up.

"Do it again, and you may just learn why they hung that name on me," the irritated Lord huffed.

"Well, this is just stupid," Billy Joe said.

Winston turned to see his partner, who was now three feet shorter, with arms the size of an infant's.

Winston fought hard to not laugh at the image. "We- ahum...we'll go get you fixed up, Baby. Bubby! I meant Bubby."

Billy Joe glared at his partner for the Freudian slip.

The guardsman sergeant, who had survived, walked around from the other side of the wrecked runabout. Clotted blood covered his head, and he looked very woozy. With a vacant expression, he saw his dead fellow guardsmen. The double blast had decimated his command.

"Look who survived," Winston said with a smile.

The sergeant nodded in greeting.

"What's your name, trooper?" Winston asked.

"Rooihemp, sir," the sergeant said. "Come, My Lord. We need to get out of here," the sergeant insisted, reaching down to help Professor Quentin up despite being walking wounded.

With a moan, the professor got to his feet. "Agreed. I do believe the time has come to take a prudent tactical withdrawal."

"Prof, is that a fancy way of saying "run fo' yo' life, y'all?" Billy Joe asked.

"Yes. Yes, it is."

"Rooihemp," Winston asked, "where's the airfield? We need to regroup. Fast."

"It'll be back this way. Means it's a little farther down the corridor, but there are airships there I recall," the sergeant said.

Winston looked down the dark passage. That was where those terrifying screams and growls had come from. He swallowed hard. "Anyone know why the emergency lights haven't come on?"

"I was just wondrin' the same," Billy Joe said.

"Things definitely are not going according to plan," the sergeant agreed.

"Does anyone else smell that?" the professor said, holding his nose.

"Phew!" Winston gasped, recoiling from the stench. "Like epoxy meets sulfur dioxide! With a big dash of metal."

"Where's it coming from?" Lord Filburt groaned, holding his nose.

"From over there," Quentin said, pointing over toward the toppled and burned tool chest. "Must be that burning dead critter."

"I gotta get out of here," Winston moaned, as Billy Joe went over to investigate the corpse of the monster.

The four surviving humans started jogging down the corridor. The Baron and Lord Filburt turned on their own pocket assistant lamps and the guardsman turned on his helmet lamp.

"Run!" Billy Joe said, and shot by them like a remote control car, skimming just above the floor as fast as his short pile of remaining nanite sand could move him.

Winston paid heed to the warning, grabbed Quentin's hand, and with a squawk of protest from the Baron, they bolted. A few dozen steps later, there was a thunderous blast from the maintenance area. Flaming wreckage bounced all around their knocked flat figures.

Winston's ears were ringing and muffled at the same time. "What was that?" he demanded.

"Them things're explosive when they die, I think," Billy Joe said, as he righted himself, again, on his stubby leg skirt.

"Everyone's okay?" Lord Filburt asked as he stood up and brushed himself off.

"Aside from the ringing ears, and that's to be expected, yeah?" Winston replied.

Thick smoke filled the corridor as the fire suppression failed to activate.

"What is going on with this place? Nothing's working?" Quentin shouted as if to accuse the facility of betrayal.

"I can't get a link to military comms. Even Lady Amanda is offline. We'll learn more once we get back to the compound," Rooihemp said.

"Then I guess we should assume nobody knows of this situation over here and we have no backup coming," Winston assessed dourly. Rooihemp nodded in agreement.

"Let's keep going and hope this chaos gives us an edge. Sergeant, lead the way," Lord Filburt ordered, and everyone fell in line behind the guardsman.

11..

Winston's chest heaved and his hands shook, making the shadows from his flashlight shiver and jump. His body rebelled against the overexertion of doing a quarter mile airborne shuffle. Rooihemp ran backwards most of the way, weapon ready, watching for anything pursuing them. Winston shot him another jealous glare. If he survived, he'd be running with the guardsmen a lot more, he promised himself. Quentin and Lord Filburt were gasping like dying horses, too.

"Well, Purg monkeys!" Winston shouted hoarsely as they neared the end of the service corridor, their flashlights illuminating the access door. Now they stood in front of a sealed garage door big enough to fit a tractor-trailer.

Thanks to the total system outage, these were powered down, too.

"This is ridiculous," wheezed Lord Filburt. "I'm not supposed to have to run like this anymore! Leave this to soldiers and children!"

Quentin could only nod his head in agreement with Lord Filburt's declaration as he gasped and held his side with a grunt.

Rooihemp looked at them all with a bit of pity and disgust. Winston sneered back at him, which prompted a headshake from the sergeant.

Exhaustion was a foreign concept to Billy Joe. He was more frustrated with his nanosand deficit and spent some time teaching himself how to share his limited stockpile between his drive skirt and arms without risking his control connections.

Physical fatigue was only part of Winston's torment. His nerves jangled like a fire alarm. The bobbing, jiggling shadows masqueraded as monsters ready to pounce, kept him dangerously anxious. He had frozen and drawn a bead on a shadow that turned out to just be his imagination so many times he lost count. His stomach was none too happy either, making him glad it was empty.

"I wish I could help out, Hoss, but that's kinda tough right now, y'know?" Billy Joe lamented, wiggling his tiny remnant arms that hardly covered the inside of his shoulder sockets.

"That's all right, Billy Joe," Quentin said. "Your sacrifice is well appreciated. We'll get you refilled back at the compound."

"Thanks, Prof," Billy Joe said with a gap-cheeked smile.

"Is there a manual door opener?" Winston demanded, as he examined the door.

"Not that I know of," said the sergeant.

"Backup power should have turned it on," Lord Filburt said as he went over to the access terminal. It was unresponsive. "Hm? It's warm. The mechanism still has power."

"But none is getting to the doors or the lights?" the professor asked.

"Seems like that's the case," Lord Filburt said. "Does anyone know much about control repair?"

"If I had my tools," Billy Joe said, then looked at his stumps, "and full arms, then I probably could have."

Winston threw up his hands and let them slap his thighs in frustration. "So, how're we going to get out? Is there a man-door?"

Another series of now familiar explosions echoed up and down the service corridor. The group spun in time to see the fireball's dying light shine around the corner from where they came. Winston and the sergeant raised their guns in case there were more.

"At least it wasn't down here with us," Lord Filburt consoled.

"Depending on the power of the shockwave. We'd be like a musketball in a plugged barrel. The blast would smash us to death against the door," Rooihemp elaborated on their potentially dire situation.

"Thank you, sergeant, for underscoring our predicament and raising our spirits," Quentin groused.

"Wait," Winston said, as he ran his hand along the surface of the door panel. "These aren't blast doors, are they, sergeant?"

Rooihemp looked back at the door for a second.

"No, sir. Just storm doors. They'd stand up to a hurricane or a vortex." Outside of black voids and meteor swarms, vortexes were the next most dangerous weather, even in the Dream. Those three dimensional tornadoes were chaos personified.

"I suppose that's a plus," Winston mused. "Can that I-beam rifle of yours be used to cut?"

"It'll burn out the battery in short order. To cut a hole big enough for us to escape takes too much power and do you want to trust our survival to just our pistols? Think that'll be enough to protect the Baron and Lord Filburt?" Rooihemp asked, leveling an irritated glance.

Winston gave the guardsman a stink-eye glare in return. "No," he growled.

"Look at this!" Quentin exclaimed. He was staring up at the ceiling. Winston shone his lamp on what the prof had spotted.

Mother of pearl mushroom folds had crept out of the air vent. The fat fungal bodies inflating, bulging out from the vent at a horror movie creep toward the floor. Each twisting stem slowly erupting with thick ears reminiscent of an oyster shell turned inside out.

"I behnging forgot about that stuff," Winston said. His mouth twisted like he was using a lemon for dentures.

"Are those fruiting bodies like a fungus, or some sort of new lifeform?" Lord Filburt wondered. He was sleepwalking toward the mysterious fungus, caught up in the fascination of discovery.

"Whatever it is," Winston interrupted, stepping between the two academics and pushing them back toward the door. "It's probably toxic, radioactive and hungry, and you are just the type of tasty treat it wants to eat. Back, back, back. Come on, back, back, back."

"Winston!" Quentin protested, writhing away from the gentle nudges. His upset inner child's personality flared up again.

"Nahq it, Quentin! I can't keep you safe if you walk into a monster's mouth to check its teeth! If you don't start caring about endangering your life, so behnging help me, I'll pistol-whip you unconscious and drag you out by your hair!" Winston exploded.

Quentin opened his mouth to rebuke Winston, then saw his companion's hand tighten around his gun's grip.

"Don't make me do it...My Lord," Winston begged.

Quentin's mouth closed, and he nodded. "You're right," he sighed. "You're right, you're right. I'm sorry."

"My Lords? Gentlemen? It's still getting bigger," Rooihemp reminded the rest. "Protect your eyes," he said, suddenly deciding.

"Oh, cheis-" Winston said and clamped his eyes shut as the guardsman swept his I-ray carbine across the ventilation grate, pruning back the dangling stems that fell to the ground. They slapped the floor more like slabs of beef than tree branches.

Lord Filburt let out a low groan of disgust.

The sound of gunfire erupted somewhere else in the complex, followed by another volley of explosions that reverberated down the corridor. Then came the startled "frripp" of the monster's rocket propulsion punctuated by fighting and shrieks that took far too long to die away.

"Poor bastards," Lord Filburt whispered.

"Those things must have caught some of Shircan's men. Poor souls," Quentin said.

"Those were close," Billy Joe speculated. "I think they're in this corridor now."

"Amazed they aren't on top of us already," Winston said.

There was a series of loud bangs from the storm doors, like a hand slapping them from outside.

"Anyone there?" a muffled voice called. "Cain't seem to git the door open."

"Ygar?" Lord Filburt said, startled at the realization. "Ygar? Is that you?"

"Course it is. I need to get a new portable terminal for the tractor. Can y'all let me in?"

"The door's powered off," Lord Filburt shouted back. "Is that one of the vintage tractors I hear?"

"Y'said I could use it fer groundskeeping!" Ygar yelled, insulted.

"Oh, thank Xiao," Lord Filburt sighed to himself, then called back through the door. "I did, and that's fine," he said. "We need your help in getting out. Time's of the essence. Can y-"

"Time's of the what?" Ygar shouted back.

"Of the- oh, nevermind! We need to get out now! Can you help us open the door? The Baron is here and needs to get to the hangar!" Lord Filburt pleaded, face tight to the door to help Ygar hear him. He looked back over his shoulder at the rest.

"The man is just infuriating," he muttered. "Gifted but...Oh!"

"I s'pose I could use the bucket to pry the door up," Ygar said.

"Yes! Do that!" Lord Filburt responded.

"One of those 'Noblesse Oblige' type of employees?" Winston asked softly.

"It would be nepotism if he was a relation," Quentin answered for Lord Filburt, "but he is no kin of mine. He's a savant of some sort in regard to maintenance. Don't expect deep conversation or fancy words from him."

The tractor's bucket bumped the door with a painfully loud bang, then an even more horrifyingly shrill scrape of metal on corundomite as the teeth began pushing at the base of the door.

"Targets!" the sergeant shouted, whipping up his I-ray carbine and opening fire. Bright red beams scribbled the far wall, revealing a small swarm of dog-sized monsters floating down the corridor toward them. He missed every one.

"Use the iron sights! They feel the smart sight's beam," Winston shouted, and pointed his pistol into the dark, waiting for his lamp to reveal his targets. They were too far away, thank Xiao.

The sergeant tipped his rifle an eighth of a turn and used the conventional sights, looking at the trio of glowing green tritium dots, trying to line them up with the small floating targets when they appeared.

"The blast must have startled them away," the sergeant said.

"Don't bet on it," Winston growled through clenched teeth.

More loud squealing as metal teeth fought to keep purchase on the door. Light leaked in from the ground into the darkness.

Both Winston and the sergeant opened fire, seeing the reflections of the monsters' glossy hides. Winston hit two, wounding but not killing them. The guardsman's I-ray scrawled all over another monster's body, popping a gas bladder of some kind in a burst of dim blue flame. It flopped on the ground, screaming. The healthy creatures fell on their wounded brood mate in a cannibalistic frenzy, turning on each other as well as the swarm went into "survival of the fittest" mode.

A distant, disconnected part of Winston's mind considered his actions. When had he gotten so brave? Normally, he'd be diving for cover and hiding. But now, he was in the thick of it and shooting.

Billy Joe slid himself next to the entrance, and oozed tendrils from his drive skirt into the gap and helped prop open the door, allowing the tractor to get a better hold. The heavy door jacked up higher.

"Come on, baby! Git'r up there!" Billy Joe hollered at the door.

The tractor whined and protested, its engine and hydraulics howling. Finally, light began streaming in as the door's notched base rose inch by inch out of the foundation.

"All of you! Out, now!" shouted Rooihemp as Billy Joe and the tractor's toothy bucket held the door open a foot off the ground.

"T'ain't wide enough yet. Just another foot," Billy Joe said, as the door rose another inch. "Give us a minute!"

"You got a few seconds!" Winston said. "Quentin! Filburt! Get ready to squirm under!"

He fired two more shots, but missed. The monsters were zig-zagging toward them like spastic minnows.

"If one of those things blows up, they all might go," warned Lord Filburt.

"The thought had crossed my mind," Winston snarled, trying to shoot another fast moving monster. His shot caroming wildly off the floor.

"Go! Go! Go!" shouted Billy Joe, who started twisting himself around on a layer of his skirt like he was doing the limbo. Quentin's thin body easily made it through.

"Your turn, sir," Rooihemp told Winston.

Winston threw himself at the gap and swam through with ease. He found himself under the big green bucket of an ancient diesel tractor and was never so happy as to smell hot grease or the stink of diesel exhaust.

"We're clear!" Winston shouted back under. Lord Filburt, Quentin and Billy Joe were behind the tractor watching the black gap, eyes wide. There were more I-beam strobes from the sergeant's carbine. They heard the guardsman's sprinting feet, and the soldier slid under.

"Drop it! Drop the door, Ygar!" Lord Filburt ordered the man with the scraggly beard and potato-like build.

"But I need a new data terminal," Ygar complained, tipping up his greasy cap to scratch a thick unruly mane of gray and brown hair.

"Do what you're told!" Filburt screamed hysterically. Hands balled into fists, looking crazier than ever. A murderous gleam in his eye.

Ygar grumbled as he threw the tractor in reverse, moving the bucket teeth the few inches back from the door, letting it fall. At the same instant, a cascade of explosions shook the ground. Flame blasted out at ankle level and buckled the door with a scary-looking bulge.

"Everyone okay?" the sergeant asked, slapping out the smoldering sparks on his clothing.

Ygar sniffed at the cloud of smoke. "Silane? What were you doin' with Silane gas in there, My Lord?" he asked Quentin.

"Is that what that smell was?" Lord Filburt asked.

"Yep," Ygar said. "Probably Hexasilane. It don't blow up so much."

"We have no time for this. Get us to the hangar right away! We must evacuate the island," Lord Filburt burst out in frustration.

"Is that what that dingin' was from the house?" Ygar said, lowering the bucket enough for everyone to step in and grab hold.

Winston looked around. His mind wanted to short out from the cognitive dissonance. The immaculate grounds revealed no sign of the horror they had just experienced. Just the hissing of the palm trees in the tropical breezes of Puala'Lolo and distant low thunder of the surf. In the distance, the Chateau aux Sceaux appeared undamaged. No sign of danger or trouble of any sort existed out here. Not even a wisp of smoke. The only indicator that anything was amiss came from the whooshing howl of airliner grav fans accelerating away replacing the joyful echoes of a distant theme park.

"Yes, Ygar. That's what the dinging was," Lord Filburt said, exasperated. "Wait," he paused, looking around. "Where is everyone else? This is the approved evacuation drill point and nobody's here?"

"Maybe they're in the hangar. I was over by the Orangerie," Ygar said, pointing off to another part of the island hidden from view. "Came over here because I needed a new data terminal. This un's broken." He held up the tablet. It, too, had a blank screen.

"We'll worry about that later," the Baron ordered. "For now, we need to regroup in the safety of the compound, so take us to the landing field, Ygar."

"As y'all want, M'Lord," Ygar said with a dip of his head as he lowered the bucket. "Hop on in."

12.

Winston doubted he'd ever ridden in any vehicle that bucked and bounced so much as the venerable tractor's bucket. It was like constant turbulence beating on his joints and making him fight to keep hold of the bucket so he didn't fall under the tires. Ygar smiled blissfully behind the wheel of the ancient piece of equipment, eyes flicking towards the Baron, searching for approval. With a radiant smile, born from obliviousness to anything he didn't want to hear, Ygar drove swiftly over to the small landing pad.

Ygar stopped close to the edge of the tarmac by the building, letting the bucket down slowly. All five bailed out of the front loader before it touched down. The small airship field was empty and the single hangar was closed.

"Doesn't look like anyone came here to take the shuttles off the island," Sergeant Rooihemp said.

"Nope," Winston said, as he walked around a little to get the wobble from the ride out of his legs, "but there's been at least one dust-off recently. They blew all the leaf litter back from those palms into the bushes, unless the gardeners were sloppy over here."

"They're over up yonder toward the mountain side doing an irrigation project in the west gardens," Ygar said. He shut the ancient machine off with a flick of his finger and climbed out of the seat with an aged groan. He walked over to the fuel pump he had parked next to and prepared to fill up the tank.

"Then someone's taken off in the last while," Winston concluded.

He gazed skyward to see the chaos of cruise blimps dispatching their ferries and shuttles to picking up their guests like bees going to and from a hive.

In the distance, specks of more airships twinkled as they came over the horizon, coming to pick up their passengers. The computer outage must have reached the theme park.

"No, no, nononono, no!" Lord Filburt's face turned pale with horror as he clearly came to the same conclusion. Winston was certain he was calculating the losses and damage to Puala'Lolo's reputation and finances as so much work sailed away.

Quentin walked over to open the main doors so they could take an airship over to the compound. "The doors on the hangar are still locked, at least," he observed and walked over to the latched padlock on the bolt.

With a press of his thumb to the network isolated padlock, he unlocked the door. Winston and Rooihemp rolled one door back, revealing the full hangar inside. A larger "longshoreman" style shuttle and a pair of two-person "flitabout" airships sat in the silent dark. Winston suspected nobody had been inside here in weeks.

"How long till you can have the shuttle ready to fly?" the sergeant asked.

"Ten minutes maybe?" Winston guessed.

"Get going. I'll keep watch," the sergeant ordered.

"Rog that," Billy Joe said, and glided over to the airship to begin the pre-flight checklist. Winston fought hard to not laugh at his partner's predicament. Seeing Billy Joe skim just inches off the ground was pure comedy to him.

"Is there anything I can help with?" Quentin asked Billy Joe as Winston climbed up into the longshoreman.

"I'm good here," Billy Joe said, as he created a precarious-looking lattice out of his drive skirt, allowing him to look into air intakes and use an arm stump to wiggle control surfaces.

"Prof!" Winston shouted from the cockpit. "You and Lord Filburt stay by the hatch. Just in case."

Quentin walked to the nose of the shuttle. "Just in case of what?" Quentin shouted at Winston through the windscreen.

As if summoned, there was a sudden whine of grav fans and a blast of fanwash into the hanger as a dropship landed on the pad, blocking them in. Rooihemp was driven back by the powerful fan wash of the combat landing. Ygar hid behind the tractor and the fuel pump.

A black, red and gold splattered combat dropship touched down. Crudely spray-painted skeletons in pirate regalia decorated the hull.

The nose art was an ancient-looking scrimshaw of the words "*Cavalier Diabolique*" which underscored an evil-looking musketeer, sword drawn. Menacing gun pods aimed loosely in the hanger's direction, but they weren't actively tracking.

"Oh, cheis," Quentin moaned.

"Get inside!" Winston hollered at the Baron. Quentin and Filburt flew up the stairs into the shuttle's passenger cabin.

Ygar stopped fueling the tractor and hung the nozzle back on the pump. A belly turret pointed curiously in his direction. He raised his hands in surrender.

Billy Joe couldn't make it to the longshoreman's hatch and had nowhere to hide but behind the tail of the shuttle.

Rooihemp raised his carbine and drew a bead on the cockpit.

"Don't be behnging stupid, cannon fodder," a voice blasted out of the dropship. Its PA system gave it a metallic ring from the high volume. Ygar slapped his hands over his ears with a cry of pain at how loud the loudspeakers were. The belly turret flashing to aim at the sergeant. The guardsman slowly raised his gun over his head, surrendering.

The ramp from the back of the dropship fell open with a dull, heavy thud on the tarmac and a group of pirates strutted out like they were on a fashion show catwalk. They acted like caricatures of pirates, promenading with a sense of invincibility toward the hanger. Hands near their weapons, or holding them loosely, ready, but not expecting any trouble.

"We were told Baron Junker was here. Produce him, and no one else needs to be hurt," their leader said as he came up to Rooihemp. With a scornful sneer, he ripped the I-ray carbine from Rooihemp's hands and sidearm from his holster.

The sergeant said nothing.

"Hey, tinman!" shouted another as he glimpsed Billy Joe peeking around the edge. Bubby ducked back like a frightened child, pretending his mother didn't see him.

"Yeah you, mechoid! Get out here or I'll cut you up for salvage!" the skypirate demanded.

Billy Joe did what he was told, little twigs of arms up in the air. The man laughed heartily when he saw the battered big indu. His torso utterly incongruous with his infantilized limbs and skirt.

The brigand gaped at the sight. "My, Xiao! Someone beat me to it!" he howled in laughter. "Top, Malcolm, Jane! Check this mechoid out!"

Three more came over to see Billy Joe skim forward. Slowly he raised himself up to his normal height on a delicate lattice of nanites which made the skypirates laugh even harder.

"Whazzamatta? Ashamed at being sawn off?" Top mocked.

"Shtoompy mechoids are sentients, too, y'know," Malcolm said. His sham defense making Billy Joe frown all the more.

From the cockpit, Winston slid to the floor and crawled back to the passenger cabin. Lord Filburt and Quentin were peeking out the windows at Billy Joe's plight.

"Are you going to help him?" Quentin asked Winston as he crawled toward the still open hatch.

"What the purg am I gonna do? One half-empty pistol and I counted at least six skypirates," Winston hissed.

"Kick their ass," Lord Filburt demanded maniacally. The stress seemed to be getting to him.

"How?" Winston glared back with a look of abject incredulity.

From outside came the muffled voice of the third skypirate "Yeah, and those short people gots no reason to live."

"Knock it off!" the dropship's PA blared. This time it was a woman's voice. "No extra killing. Especially that one. Secure the prisoners, catch the Baron and let's vamoose!"

Winston crept up to peek over the bottom edge of a window and saw Sergeant Rooihemp kneeling on the ground, a gun to his head.

"Check out the shuttle," the PA woman ordered, guns now trained on it. "Maybe he's hiding in there. Come on out, Baron Junker. We won't harm you." Her voice was much more kind this time.

"Yeah, just a bit of friendly ransom," Lord Filburt grumbled.

"What's a little bounty hunting among friends, right?" Winston griped. His mind wheeled trying to formulate an escape plan for them all, but only coming up with solutions that would end up with him vaporized.

"Well, behng it," Lord Filburt blurted. His face getting a blotchy red. "If you're not willing to do something, I will." The nobleman stood up and stomped aft and threw back the accordion door to the stewardess station.

"Quentin, get in here, and stay put till we leave the ground or we come and get you." There was no negotiating with Lord Filburt's tone. No give at all.

"Oh, Nutty," Quentin moaned, but he obeyed his friend.

"That's right," Lord Filburt said as he slid the door closed, making sure it locked. "And pilot? Are you with me or must I do everything alone?" he asked Winston.

"I'm in like Flynn," he said, regretting it.

"Good, get behind those seats near the cockpit, and be ready to ambush them when I go," Lord Filburt ordered.

With an angry toss, he slammed open a mini fridge and pulled out some bottles. With a pair in each hand, he walked to the hatch opening, and lobbed them out to smash on the hard hanger floor, then quickly ducked back into the stewardess' galley.

Winston could hear the hard slapping of several pairs of running feet. He tasted copper, and his palms were so slicked with sweat he felt as if the pistol would slip out.

A faint tilt of the shuttle and changes in the light, signaled the skypirates boarding the shuttle. Carefully, the first two entered, behind the cover of the seats.

Something smelled like it was burning.

A second pair of shadows joined the first, and two more hostiles stepped in, guns raised, ready for an ambush.

The stewardess's galley screen whipped back and a bare-chested Lord Filburt burst forth with a shriek, two flaming liquor bottles raised over his head. His voluminous gut sagging over his belt from decades of good eating and comfort.

"You want the Baron?" he screamed. "Come! Let's burn together!" The pirates were caught between laughter and shock at the sight of Lord Filburt charging them.

Certain that was his cue, Winston popped up from behind the passenger seats, braced the pistol on a headrest, and fired two times before his magazine went dry.

Both standing skypirates went down screaming. The musketballs smashed through a seat and into the hip of one and exploded the shoulder of the other.

The two brigands who had crouched on the floor were now entangled with their fallen comrades as Lord Filburt attempted to stomp them to death. Shrieking like a madman, he kept shoving the fiery end of the burning bottles into their faces. It was as if he was doing a Morris Dance as a martial art, dipping down to burn them with the flaming bottles as he went.

The trapped men wailed in terror and pain, squirming to get out from under their wounded, screaming cohorts. As they struggled to escape, they fell down the hatchway's retractable steps into the hanger, landing in a heap, slapping their burning clothing. Winston heard several more of their crewmates on the way. The smack of musketballs shook the shuttlecraft. U-rays cut chunks of the windscreen in crazy scrawls as the reinforcements fired on the run. Little pock marks from pulse I-rays lanced through the entire airship like a sewing machine needle.

One water-tuned U-ray hit Lord Filburt's thigh, erupting in a steaming spray of flash-boiled blood and tissue. With a surprised grunt, he threw the Molotov cocktails out the hatch, trying to block the skypirates by igniting the alcohol spread across the ground. The bottles bounced away on impact and rolled around unbroken.

"Cheis," Lord Filburt groaned as he fell into a seat. "Those bottles were tougher than I thought."

Winston took a chance to get a skypirate's firearm. Just as he reached for it, he saw the muzzles of the boarding party's reinforcements pointing at him through the hatch. He jerked back just in time as a volley of musketballs, U-rays and even a squirtgun loaded with liquid metal fired. The ultra high-pressure liquid metal shredded the inside of the cabin wall, chopping large chunks out of the interior and tearing the unarmored hull open.

"Stop shooting you cretins!" the PA blared. "We're not killing anyone! We're here to collect the Baron and go! Are you trying to behng this up for the captain? Nahq it!" There was the screech of the mic being thrown down in frustration.

Winston realized he had a chance. If they can't kill, he might be lucky enough to win this fight.

Hah! Who are you kidding? He chided himself. This is a suicide run and you know it.

"Do it," Filburt whispered, and flashed Winston a ghastly smile set in a waxy complexion. "Don' worry 'bout me. J'st keep Quentin...safe." He grunted again, his hand pressed hard against his ruptured thigh, blood dripping on the floor.

Winston was sure Lord Filburt would bleed out if he couldn't get a medical kit to patch him up fast. Before he could focus on him, Winston had to stop the skypirates, and the only way they could flee was if he took over their dropship.

That was assuming the monsters didn't show up first.

"Kick th'r azzez fr' me," Nutty slurred, clenching a fist in encouragement before slumping bonelessly into the chair.

"Well," Winston whispered to the fading Filburt, "ya gotta die of something."

Winston felt the slight tilt of the shuttle again as a new skypirate climbed the hatchway steps. When the intruder reached the top, Winston stepped into the doorframe.

"Sorry, buddy. This ain't your flight."

Winston's foot lashed out, catching the startled brigand square in the face, knocking him backwards, launching him headfirst into the pack of his close following press gang, bowling them over.

Winston leapt from the top stairs, landing among them. A stun baton whipped at Winston's head. He power parried the attacker's arm, putting him into an elbow lock. With a quick twist, he snapped the raider's arm and bent it backwards, ramming the baton into his bare neck with a crackling pop of electricity. The man was out like a light.

A wired buccaneer lifted Winston off the ground in a bear-hug. Winston slapped the stun baton against the attacker's side with a flick of his wrist. Nothing happened. The wired pirate was immune, grounded from the Baton's danger. Winston's other hand brushed the skypirate's holster with the tip of his fingers as the buccaneer applied another breath stealing crush.

Winston's fingers scratched the man's pistol just loose enough from its holster that he was able to hook the trigger. A three-shot pulse of U-rays blew through both of the wired man's legs. Winston dropped like a cat, the pulse pistol now in his control. His wiry assailant crumpled, howling in pain. Winston used a spin kick as a coup de grace to the man's temple, silencing him.

He spun around to face his next attacker. A baton smashed through the pulse pistol, and the impact shot a stinging jolt up his arm, numbing his hand. The baboon primatoid shrieked, revealing terrifying fangs to Winston, who shoved the stun baton into its mouth and gave a savage uppercut. The primatoid's teeth shattered, the baton discharged its capacitor as the blow broke the weapon and fried the inside of the splice's mouth.

Winston suddenly saw stars and the hanger ceiling, unsure of how he got there. His head throbbed from a blow from behind. A woman's arms snaked around his neck, and she nestled right up into his side in a judo submission hold, choking him out. The crook of her arm pinched off his carotid artery and windpipe.

Winston floundered against the agile woman's skilled grasp, but could not break it. He tried to throw punches at her face, but she shoved herself cheek to cheek to immobilize Winston's head against his own shoulder, rendering him unable to strike back.

"Gotcha now, you cheis-behnger," she hissed as he flailed away.

"Huk...huk..." Winston tried to speak, but couldn't. She'd cut off all air and blood flow to his brain. In a couple seconds, he'd be out. His arm wriggled under her, trying to gain leverage, but she squirmed around, keeping her advantaged angle.

Pinned between her ribcage and the floor, his hand found hard, round spheres of grenades. Marshaling all his waning strength, he grabbed hold with his numb finger and jerked. He felt something come free and lifted it to dangle the item in front of her face. The world grew dark and small as his consciousness slipped farther away.

"Grenade!" the woman screamed. To Winston, she sounded miles away despite it being right in his ear. She released him and sat up, thrashing to get the bandoleer off her body, lifting the grenades over her head.

Pain from oxygen starvation roared in as her hold released and Winston's blood flow restored the last of his strength. He flipped up his legs to kick her away from him. Both feet struck her chest. She flew backwards and landed in a heap a few feet away, half tangled in her bandoleer.

Unable to stand up himself, Winston rolled, as best as he could, away from her, hoping it was far enough. He shoved his face into the ground and covered his ears, waiting for the heat and pain to wash over him.

Nothing happened.

He was not sure how long he had lain there getting his strength back when there came the sound of metallic clicking. Someone walked slowly toward him.

"My, my, my, Flyboy. You never fail to impress, do you?" said a woman. Her speech tickled his ear with familiar whiskey-burned alto tones.

Winston's limbic system itched like crazy, instantly aroused. Anger and shock boiled up in its wake as he remembered that sensation.

His eyes slowly rose upward, taking in the owner of that voice which he never expected to hear again. Two feet shod in impossibly long metal heels, weapons as much as they were decorations, posed in front of him. The black gloss of smartex and pandifico armor plates glided up those caricature perfect legs and hips. The armor displayed just as much as it contained her majestic breasts. Her corseted neo-swashbuckling, crazy-sensual, pirate queen fetish outfit acted as a tactical harness. A big feathered broad-brimmed hat topped off the ensemble of dangerous sensuality.

All the fight left in Winston drained away as he saw Holly towering over him, looking down like a praying mantis sizing up her next mate.

"Miss me?" she cooed and reached down to pick him up.

13..

"I knew you weren't dead!" exploded Winston. His soul felt like it was being ripped into emotional confetti. Anger, joy, arousal and loathing swirled through him as the amazon nanoborg who had tormented his life lifted him to his feet.

"Lady Nightshade, you know this dronepleb?" the grenade woman asked.

Winston, a full four inches shorter than Holly, looked right into her smiling lips that seemed to grow redder and glossier with each second that she gazed at him, like a freshly fed vampire.

"Lady Nightshade?" Billy Joe wondered aloud as he came around the corner of the mangled shuttlecraft where he had hid since the fight began. Winston didn't blame him for doing so. He couldn't have helped.

"Well, hey there, short stack," Holly said. "Yes, it's me, Lady Nightshade," her voice was chipper, as if glad to see him, but her eyes were hard as flint. "Remember?" There was an iced warning in that last word.

"Now Miss H- Nightshade, how could I ever forget a passenger like you?" Billy Joe smoothed over.

"And, yes, Dungle. Me and Flyboy here have a rather short and bumptious history."

Winston could hear the light squeak of her smartex fingers rub his neck as she adjusted the collar. Her smell mingling with her perfume, the dance of her fingers straightening out his Hawaiian shirt set his brain on fire.

"Haven't we..." she paused a pair of heartbeats before breathing, "Winston?"

Even without the limbic manipulator, Winston's mouth went dry. His resolve and confusion began turning to mush. Her skin seemed saturated with color since he last saw her, and the faintest hint smoother. Newer skin in a splash pattern across her face rendered her even more ethereal. Her eyes a milky jade in dark smokey pools.

"Mmm-hm!" he said, too scared to open his mouth for fear of what might come out. The two leading choices were ill-chosen words or vomit.

"Why didn't we blow up?" the grenade girl asked the open floor, looking at her bandoleer.

"Pardon me a moment, Flyboy. I need a consult with the staff," Holly said and brushed heavily by him with her hip. The kneeling woman who almost killed them all held up the bandoleer to Holly.

Holly snatched the belt of flywheel grenades from her hands and looked at the capacitor indicator. Nodding to herself in growing irritation, Holly drew back and began whipping the grenadier mercilessly with the bandolier like a scourge.

"You! Didn't! Charge! The! Behnging! Grenade! Cores!" she shouted with every blow.

Two other skypirates quietly traded money. One smirked while the other shook his head.

Holly wrapped the strap around the woman's neck in a quick, cruel noose and hauled her to her feet, half hanging her. "That! Is why you didn't kill our target or your crewmates! You slab of worthless meat!"

Holly flung the woman by the strap toward the dropship. She skidded to a halt, covered with patches of road rash to her arms, face covered in rising welts and darkening bruises, gasping for breath from her near execution.

"Get onboard, strap in and say nothing!" Holly shouted, "Piss me off again and I'll have you keelhauled through a gravel storm!" Grenade girl did what she was told and limped back to the dropship.

Winston's mouth hung open as the sensual sensations blasted out of him faster than a musketball by Holly's violent attack.

"Sorry, Flyboy. Trouble with the staff. Where were we?" Holly said in satirized human resources talk as she glided back towards him. Winston took a step back, taking a loose ready stance, hands loose at his side, waiting for a fight.

Holly stopped, put her hands prayerfully in front of her lips, and gave a sad frown.

"Aww, come now, Winston," she begged with a sappy pout. "Are you still that afraid of me?"

"He is if he knows what's good for him," one of the betting skypirates snarked. Holly snapped her onyx fingers and pointed at him, but never took her eyes off of Winston's.

The mouthy skypirate shut up.

"Bubby! Do you know why I'm here all of a sudden?" Holly sighed, striding past Winston and over to the mangled mechoid.

"I'm not sure, Miss Nightshade," Billy Joe answered slowly, careful to use her new name, "But we don't got time for playing around. Them monsters is coming, sure as shooting."

"Monsters?" Holly stroked the scuffs of the indu's wounds, tutting at them like a sympathetic nurse. "Is that how you got these boo-boos, Crusher?" she taunted.

"Why do you want the Baron? Ransom wasn't your game, I thought," Winston said to her back.

She looked over her shoulder to give Winston a full wattage smile.

"Close, Flyboy. No gold star for you," she purred. "Baron Junker is not my goal. He is the means to which I'll get what I do want. He is master of Puala'Lolo, and by extension, all his servants. That group now includes you. And your Bubby. And the *Sierra Madre*. Surprise!" She gave a half curtsy, arms spread wide, like a game show model presenting a new airship.

"So?" Winston said. "Can we quit the games? We don't have time." Then added with a spike of spite, "Just like on Blaugarten. Remember?"

"Oh, I definitely remember that...Winston. Don't think I've forgotten," Holly growled, her eyes flaring bright red with anger.

"Yeah, well..." Winston had a hitch in his thoughts as her lips turned black, surrounding her smile of perfect white teeth. "We still gotta git. Your dropship is the best we can do right now. So, can we please?"

"Ooh! With a 'please', no less. Don't worry. We'll get there soon enough. I needed to collect my last trump card. Having your master at hand will make it much easier to get back what is mine," Holly said. She sauntered up to the shuttlecraft hatch and leaned up.

"Xiao nahq it!" Winston shouted at Holly. "Quit behnging around, and let's get out of here. Wait? What do I have that's yours?" Winston demanded.

Holly's disappointed roll of her eyes made it clear what she thought of his question.

"Baron Junker? Professor? Would you mind being a sweetheart and coming out here? I'd like to speak with you!" she called into the airship.

Winston grunted and took a step toward her before he realized it. He felt like she pulled him toward her by his brainstem. A violent shake of his head cleared his mind. That minx learned a new trick with her limbic manipulator! Was it some sort of subconscious suggestion mode, or did it trigger a strong desire to trust? What was that sensation?

Quentin poked his head out from around the corner. "Is it safe?" came the professor's voice.

From the rear of the hanger, there was the sound of squealing, like a cat's claws scratching porcelain, then a loud bang as an air duct vent fell to the ground. Winston saw a monster the size of a rabbit float into the building. This one had two lobster like claws on spindly arms protruding from just behind its jaws. In full light, the creature was even uglier. Greasy charcoal skin dripped some sort of steaming mucus. Glassy fins refracted a dim flickering glow like fiber optics from somewhere in its body.

"Cheis," Winston shouted and stepped forward to pick up the fallen wiry's pulse pistol from the ground. Holly drew both her pistols, aiming one at Winston, and the other toward the noise.

"Get back!" Winston shouted. All those who could scatter did so in every direction. Quentin ducked back into the mangled shuttle.

Holly fired before Winston was able, and the creature jerked and twitched out of the way of her smart sights. Her eyes widened in shock at the miss. Winston tipped his pulse pistol at an angle and fired down the barrel. The three-shot burst of

U-rays punched holes through the monster as it readied to charge Holly.

In the dim light of the hangar, they saw a near invisible blue burst of flame, then felt a flash of horrible heat. The thing hit the ground like a popped children's toy, and began a skin-twitching ululating wail as it floundered on the ground.

Holly took aim as it flopped like the dying fish on the shore.

"No, don't!" Winston screamed, but her musketball was already in flight. It smacked into the sparkling diamond belly that smashed like a Christmas ornament, spinning the body into some maintenance equipment.

They were too close. Winston threw himself at Holly, even though her second pistol pointed at his heart.

The monster exploded.

She pulled the trigger.

Winston's world went black.

<><><>

His head ringing, Winston came to. There was a tickling sensation coming from inside his right ear and that side of his face felt cold. Something warm, smooth and sticky was below him.

"Mind getting off my boob?" Holly asked.

He opened his eyes and found himself on top of Holly. His head had been nestled face down into her cleavage.

With a jerk, Winston got up on his knees. His blood smeared all over her armored chest, almost invisible on the slick black surface, the rest soaked into the fibers of her costume bolero jacket and outlandish hat. He patted his face and found a cut on his scalp. Directly above the two, where they had been standing, the hull of one of the flitabouts was perforated from tools turned into shrapnel by the exploding creature. Holly looked unharmed. Barely ruffled from the blast.

"Ruined," she grumbled as she saw her stained jacket.

"Sorry," Winston mumbled. "Wait. You shot at me!"

"And missed, it seems. Stupid shockwave," she granted, lifting herself up on her elbows. "You tried to save me again."

"Yeah?"

"Don't think that's going to get anywhere with me," Holly groaned and got to her feet.

"Xiao on a cracker, Lady!" Winston grumbled. "If you don't take the cake."

"Winston?" Came Quentin's voice from inside the shuttle, not revealing a hair.

"What? Oh, yeah! It's safe for the moment, Prof," Winston said and coughed, getting to his own feet. The remaining skypirate gang was also getting up.

"What the cheis was that?" Top demanded.

"Those are the monsters that don't got a name yet," Billy Joe said, coming back. He had made it all the way to the landing pad before the explosion. He zig zagged from small bits of burning wreckage, putting them out by smothering them with his nanite skirt.

"There he is! Good morning, Baron Junker," Holly said, switching on her obsequious courtly mannerisms. There was a faint rumble of confusion and irritation from the other skypirates. Even Winston rolled his eyes at her act.

"Lord Filburt is bleeding badly. I have the first aid pack on him, but we need to get him to the compound right away," Quentin pleaded.

"And we shall, My Lord," Holly agreed. "I'm confident Lady Amanda will be able to patch him up, and my fellow shipmates, in no time. Come with me and we'll get you and Lord Filburt there on my ship."

"If you think you're going to go see Lady Amanda, you've got another think coming," Winston said.

"Darling, yet again, you are in no position to negotiate anything. As you've said, we've no time to play around, and don't forget, Lord Filburt needs urgent care." Holly's voice was cordial poison toward Winston. He cursed himself for forgetting this woman was as treacherous, flighty and deadly as the sky.

"Dungle, Malcolm, Jane! Help Lord Filburt and we'll get the rest of you lot patched up as well when we're at the Junker compound."

"You are very kind, Lady...Nightshade?" Quentin asked, unsure of the name.

She nodded with a coy smile aimed at the Baron. "Yes, My Lord."

"Excellent. Oh! You have met my sister-in-law? Lady Amanda? She ran Puala'Lolo in my absence," Quentin said as he came out of the shuttlecraft. She took the nobleman's hands as he descended the last steps. Her soaring stature towered over him by nearly a foot.

"We are acquainted well enough, My Lord. In fact, all three of us have a lot to talk about once we're safe from whatever this infestation is." Holly's voice was like burning oil over water as her eyes fell upon Winston once again.

14..

Lady Amanda watched the sun climb higher in the digital bright blue sky till it reached its apogee. A few pixelated clouds skipped by as if driven by spastic data transfer speeds. Outside the truck stop, the traffic on the twin highways of trucks was roaring. Non-stop lines of vehicles took turns passing through the intersection. Inside the bright white, copper and sea-foam green diner, everything smelled of maple syrup, hamburger and bacon. Every stool and chair was full of even more exotic versions of Motherroad's avatars. All the gas pumps were full of cars and light trucks, while big rigs fueled up at the string of islands out back.

Amanda couldn't even guess as to what those avatars represented in Mother's code, let alone why it was necessary to be represented here, but it all seemed tied together with her rebuilding process. An instant version of a "percentage completed" bar. In the parking lot a luxury car pulled up to the diner's car spots. Those were rare. Must be some sort of special program, Amanda guessed, as a new version of Mother got out. This avatar dressed like an elite business woman on her way to a meeting.

Her crisp suit was in a soft dove grey with a hint of holographic stitching. The jacket's big shoulders gave an exaggerated tapering silhouette to her severe patent court shoes. A brilliant white camisole was painfully bright in the sunlight, accessorized with a ghost pearl necklace, and a copper, platinum and emerald pin of her corporate logo on her lapel. Cinched around her waist was a bright copper belt that matched her severe pumps, gloves, and mirrored sunglasses. Her silver blonde hair swept back in a sharp wave to a tight bun.

Amanda leaned over to tip the Venetian blinds out of the way and watched this new avatar come into the diner. "Corporate Executive Mother" walked directly to Amanda in her booth with long purposeful strides. Mother stopped at the booth and looked down at her with a hard analytical gaze, while her expression showed she found what she saw as wanting.

"I don't know if you're brave, cursed, foolish or all of the above coming in here like this," she said without preamble.

Lady Amanda gave a little jerk back at the insult.

"It doesn't matter." Mother dismissed the coming rebuke with a wave of her hand and slid into the booth opposite of her. The waitress brought a vodka gimlet the instant she settled in her seat.

"I thought you avatars didn't need to drink," Amanda said snidely.

"We don't. Same way we don't need to eat, drive trucks, smoke or anything else you see. I wanted to try this conceit in order to better relate to you "biomes" by engaging in your typical vices," Mother said, with the dataoid slur toward biological beings, and raised her glass. "Cheers."

She drained the glass in a single gulp, cocktail onion and all. She smacked her lips once, looked at the glass, and held it up for a fresh drink. The waitress whisked it away.

Amanda shook her head in overwhelmed astonishment.

"You wanted a smaller, less disruptive, but still functional version of me. An avatar with access to the last information Motherroad had before my kernel's demise. Lucky you. You got the avatar that worked with Winston. That means I know all about the mess you got us into."

"You can actually do that? Control which avatar you use?" Amanda was astonished.

Mother squinted and quirked her mouth in consternation. "Of course, I can. What kind of academic are you? Don't you know about this with your umpteen billion degrees?" Mother snapped as her next drink showed up.

"My knowledge implants don't include perfect recall, you know," Amanda shot back.

"Not my problem. Now fill me in, so I can make a plan of action once I get us both back online," Mother said, sniffing the martini. "This is a no. Waitress? Something else." She held out her drink, which was picked off instantly. "Do go on, dear. I'll think while I decide what I like to drink."

The waitress brought a whiskey Manhattan. Amanda stared at the avatar trying to work out what she was seeing in this fun-house of an instance where everything was familiar, but nothing was what it seemed. Mother must not have approved of Amanda's inability to get past the strangeness of this interaction.

Mother took a sip, then a swig of the drink, shrugged and put the glass down. "I said, 'Go on', dear. Time is short and we have lots to do."

Amanda explained the events since arriving in Nova Tortuga, meeting with Commodore D. P. Roberts and the solving of Mother's message. She talked about the therapy she put Winston through to repair his brainburn injury and subsequent downloads.

"Hold up there a moment," Mother said, lifting a finger, stopping Amanda's rundown. "Let's not gloss over the money shot here. What do you mean by 'additional downloads', vis-à-vis Winston?"

"Keeping Quentin safe at home wasn't in the cards, so I had to come up with an alternative plan. Protection while he was about. Since Winston and Billy Joe needed work, and I had need of savvy, dream-wise individuals like them, I just did to Winston what you did to Billy Joe," Amanda said matter-of-factly.

"What do you think I did to Billy Joe?" Mother said, a hint of danger in her voice.

"You downloaded combat routines in him so he could act like a waroid, too," Amanda said.

Mother thought for a second. "Ah. That."

She shook her head. "What I did with Billy Joe is not the same. A long time ago, my company installed those routines with his permission. When the job was done, he returned to his previous state in accordance with the law. All those mods got locked away and deactivated. I never once lied to or violated him regarding what was done. After all, he is- well...was one of my employees and signed off on the customization for a limited term job. This was well before he partnered up with Winston. You may not think it, but I do respect mechoid personal autonomy."

"Oh?" Amanda wasn't sure what to make of that revelation. Perhaps what she had done was a bridge too far.

"Winston, on the other hand, I hired him in as an owner/operator subcontractor. Do you know why he's avoided implanting a data jack? He's always been very independent and anti-modification." Mother tapped her fingernail on the formica tabletop, hard. "Very."

"He never noticed-" Amanda tried to explain when Mother shook her head in a hard dismissal of her rationalization.

"You did these downloads with his knowledge?" Mother fixed a prickly stare on the over-enthusiastic scientist.

"Well...it didn't do any harm," Amanda squirmed under Mother's glare.

"Oh, I'm sure it's going to do some harm when he learns what you did, Missy," Mother said, crossing her arms and glaring at the noblewoman. Amanda felt three inches tall.

"Were any of these mods combat related?" Mother asked, taking another drink.

"Yes," Amanda mumbled. Although she was able to do such things, she had never for a second considered if she should do something like this to a man against his will, for she didn't think about anything beyond her own desires in this respect.

"Xiao wept," Mother said and pinched the bridge of her nose in anguish. "You're only one step better and three steps to the right of that psychopath, O'Chaudry!"

"Hey!" Amanda bristled.

"Zip it!" Mother snarled. "It's exactly that! What O'Chaudry would have done was at least honest and forthright. You used your noble ends to excuse an objectively evil act! Purg, that's Xiao level mendacity. For example, how'd you like me to overwrite your brain with my code? I can do it with a snap of my fingers. If it's evil when it's done to you, then it's evil if done to someone else."

It was a long time before Amanda could speak, as the shame for what she'd done slammed home. "I see what you mean," she whispered.

"You remember that the next time you think another sentient being's your lab rat. Now, you best tell me what mods you did to his brain, and pray you didn't mess with his ethical framework, otherwise nothing I can do will save you from the vengeance Winston will visit upon you and your house."

15..

The dropship *Cavalier Diabolique* skimmed low over the surf of Puala'Lolo toward the Junker's palatial compound. Quentin sat in the co-pilot's seat, looking around at the controls like an excited child whose father took him to work.

In the conversational lull, Winston listened to the radio traffic as it drifted back to them from the cockpit's speakers. It was chock-full of ship-to-ship chatter, trying to figure out why ground control had disappeared. No trafficnet positioning links, no tower, nothing. Not even automated backups.

He looked out the window. Some more of the big tourist airships started pulling away, while others had dispatched their landing shuttles for their guests, readying for departure.

Like it or not, this was going to be the financial disaster Lord Filburt feared. Whatever plans Doctor A and Professor Q had in mind were going up in smoke.

Winston noticed Holly's fellow crew mates gave her a wide berth, cramming themselves into the end seats with the wounded on the deck between them, giving the three the illusion of privacy.

Winston finally gave in and stared at Holly as she sat across the aisle from him, legs crossed. Her heel swung like a conductor's baton in time to the music playing in her head. Like a cat in a sunbeam, she looked back through heavy-lidded eyes.

"You fell overboard," Winston challenged her look.

"I did," she answered softly. "And you came looking for me, too," her smile smacked of satisfaction at Winston's failed attempt to save her.

"You saw?" Winston said.

"Mmmhmmmm," she murmured seductively.

"We couldn't find you," Billy Joe added.

"This jolly lot picked me up a few hours before you arrived, responding to my emergency beacon," she explained, stretching out her arms on the rests to the seats on either side of her, crossing her ankles. "They found me floating, unconscious, near that amphiboid corpse and brought me aboard."

"That's why we couldn't find your beacon," Billy Joe said, connecting the dots.

She nodded in confirmation and added, "While you were searching for me, I was unconscious in their sick bay, but I saw the sensor logs after I recovered."

Winston couldn't help but squirm at her tone. Even without the limbic manipulator, his feelings toward her fizzed and roiled under her smug gaze.

"I did what any self respecting airman would do," Winston mumbled humbly.

"Ohhhh...and we know about your self-respect. It's such a big thing for you, too," Holly purred.

Then the verbal claws came out. "How's Valerie?"

Winston's anger flared but the intended rebuke died in his mouth as his heart became ice.

Holly's eyes twinkled at the direct hit.

The other skypirates strapped into their seats on the other side of the airship leered wolfishly at him. His eyes flicked over to their hungry stares.

"Oh, yes! I much prefer this subject," she said with a crooning lilt and leaned forward expectantly. "Did it take a few days or weeks to get back into your home instance to visit? How is the little woman? Has she noticed any changes in you lately?"

"Changes?" The word hung in the air between them like a kite tethered in a windstorm.

She gave him a mocking scowl. "You know precisely what I'm talking about. There's no use hiding it from me." Holly's voice rose and fell in sing-song amusement.

"In the short while we've been in each other's company again, I have noticed some big differences. You've changed a lot since I had you face down on that container floor," she teased, tapping a finger next to an elegantly winged eye.

The skypirates didn't even have the common courtesy to hide their lurid interest in Winston's torture at Holly's hands.

"You say lots of things. What's that supposed to mean?" Winston glared at her, frustrated by her insinuations, trying to pour psychological cement on his own doubts.

"You mean..." Holly looked shocked. "Bubby? You realize, don't you?"

"Dunno what yer talking about, Miss H-Nightshade," Billy Joe said.

Her brow furrowed for a second with intense scrutiny as he caught himself. Then she brightened and burst out in jolly musical laughter.

"Oh, this is too precious!" she laughed gaily, stomping her feet, unable to contain herself. "Oh, oh, yes, cheis yes! This is going to be so amusing!"

"What are you babbling about?" Winston shouted at her. His fists balled up.

"Oooh," she cooed. "Aren't you the tough customer all of a sudden?"

The dropship darkened abruptly, leaving them in the dim artificial light of the cabin lamps.

"Ah! Don't worry, you'll learn what I'm talking about soon enough," Holly said, alerted by her pilot's cybercom. "We're here."

There was a gentle descent and bump as the dropship landed inside the compound's industrial lab hanger. Holly popped her restraints and stood up with a stretch.

She went to the cockpit, sashaying between her crew to collect Quentin, and gave orders to the rest. "Take the wounded to the medical lab. Looks like some sort of mass outage, so don't expect much help. Take extra care with Lord Filburt here. He's in a delicate state. Fashion some litters if you must, and don't trust the auto-medics to work. Malcolm, Jane, with me, and we'll escort the Baron and his entourage to see Lady Amanda so we can take care of business and get out of here."

With orders given, Holly escorted Quentin out of the dropship, like he was the nerd who scored a date with his crush, the prom queen.

Winston glowered at her as she strutted past, a train of skypirates behind her, giggling like hyenas.

When the Baron and his entourage exited the skypirate dropship, the skypirates split up. One group whisked the desperately wounded Lord Filbert down the hallway to the medical clinic. Billy Joe went to the maintenance station to refill his nanosand for his arms and drive skirt. The remaining three, with Holly on the Baron's arm, marched down to Lady Amanda's office. A few yards from her office door, the lights came back on.

"Ah! It seems they fixed whatever was wrong with the network," Quentin said happily. "Hope that helps Chief Shircan get things under control back at the library."

Suddenly, Rooihemp grabbed his head as loud audio spiked into his ear. The security comms exploded with security breach alarms and an abduction warning.

"Stand down. Cancel anti-abduction response. Proceed Charlie Delta Three. Repeat, cancel anti-abduction response!" Rooihemp ordered into the comms.

A chorus of compliance came back over the comm, but Winston suspected that there was a security net being cast about them. The skypirates couldn't escape without a fight if things went sideways.

At the end of the hall, he saw two periscopes peek around the corner. The houseguards were at the ready. Quentin opened the door of the lab to find his sister-in-law at her desk, staring into space, with a frozen horrified look.

"Amanda?" Quentin called softly. Her eyes snapped onto him, then flitted about, taking in his entourage. The look grew more panicked till it burst like a wave.

"Oh? Oh! Thank Xiao you're all right," she gasped. Her chair knocked over as she rushed around her desk and hugged him. Quentin laughed nervously for a moment, then hugged her back.

She moved back to arm's length, looking him over like an overprotective mother examining her child. "I couldn't forgive myself if something happened."

"Aman- Amanda! Stop fussing!" Quentin said, grabbing her arms, trying to calm her.

"It wasn't a sure thing for a while, Doc," Winston said. "But Shircan and the rest of us got him through. Lord Filburt took a purg of a shot though, thanks to these numbbehngers." He hooked a thumb back toward the skypirates who were standing against the back wall of her lab office watching, but ready for action. Again, he saw the house guard's periscopes looking through the glass.

Amanda could not meet Winston's eyes as she nodded a thank you to him. Then she recognized Holly.

"Nice to see you again, My Lady," Holly said cordially.

"Ah," Amanda said with stiffening formality. "I am glad to see you survived. Thank you for all you did on the *Sierra Madre*," she added, her face now hardened.

The thanks she gave may have been sincere, but it was filtered through a ceramic mask of diplomacy. The awkward pause between the women filled the room like a foul smell.

"Yes. Well, I can tell I caught you at a bad time, so I will keep my business here short," Holly said, echoing the quality of Lady Amanda's thanks. "First things first. Where are my cases? I'll have them now and leave you to take care of whatever is going on in private."

"Your cases," Amanda repeated, looking befuddled for a minute.

"Aw, cheis," Winston said, rubbing his mouth and chin. He'd forgotten about them with all that had been going on.

"And the penny drops!" Holly turned to look back at him. "That's right, Flyboy. You didn't think I'd come all this way just to behng with your head, did you?"

"The thought occurred to me, actually," Winston said. His acerbic wit generated a nasty sarcastic smile back at him from her.

"You mean those armored, biometrically sealed cases, with the null-scan linings inside scratched up corundumite casings?" Amanda asked.

"Those would be the ones," Holly agreed.

"I sent them over to the decryption lab at Quentin's research library," Amanda said.

"You did what?" Winston shouted.

"Quentin has code-breakers and other cryptographic cypher machines in his library. It seemed reasonable that it would be a better place to open them. So, they're over in his cryptography office," Amanda explained.

Quentin held up a finger to excuse himself, went over to a terminal and started working.

Winston gave a loud groan and kicked a trashcan across the room. He glared at Holly, then turned away in disgust, turning his gaze out the windows and into the hanger.

"What's your problem?" Holly snarled at him.

"Other than you being here? It means we can't get rid of you till you get your cases." He watched the giant fabricator inch higher. It was the first time he noticed his new ship's base and the design was already radically different from what he expected.

"Yeah? So?" Holly said sharply, as she walked over and got in Winston's face. Her color pulsing eyes no longer intimidated him. They were just irritating now.

"You've no behnging clue what kinda trouble that's going to cause," he ranted.

"She don't get her cases, Cap'n don't get paid," one of the skypirates spoke up. Then, in a more sinister tone, said, "He will get paid." His fellow crewmates nodded in agreement.

Winston sneered at the skypirate, "You don't get it. You're in a horror movie now. Adding this distracting side-quest is going to get people killed!"

The skypirate scoffed at Winston's vehemence. Disgusted, he turned his back on the foolhardy brigand and Holly.

"It's gonna be hard enough to deal with those floating monsters from purg that're coming out of the air vents over there, killing people. Then there's that naqh fungus eating everything it touches. I don't even wanna know what'll happen if it touches a living being," Winston explained.

"What do you mean by 'eating'?" Holly demanded. He could hear her frustration that her physical presence didn't cow him anymore and he dared turn his back on her.

"Are these the fungus and creatures Chief Shircan told me about?" Amanda asked.

"Yeah. Some weird mother-of-pearl looking garbage. It's made out of silicone, we think. Something you're familiar with. The stuff grows on everything and is all over the research library complex," Winston said.

"And you put my cases in the middle of your mess?" Holly exclaimed, disregarding his cheap shot.

Winston ignored her.

With a sudden jerk, his world spun around and he found himself literally nose to nose with Holly. Her eyes were cycling through color like a psychotropic swirl. In a flash of lucidity, Winston saw through her act and glimpsed the fear at her core. What was it that scared her so?

"Nothing better happen to them," she threatened.

Winston was sick of being manhandled and gave her a headbutt, knocking her back. Her mouth dropped open. He hoped to not have to repeat the move because that hurt, bad.

"Back off! I didn't do it," he snarled and swiped his arm in a circle, breaking free of her grasp then thrust a finger towards Lady Amanda. "She did!"

"Be nahqing glad I found where you hid your cases before we disassembled the *Sierra Madre*. They almost became part of that, out there," Winston said, stabbing another finger toward the nanofabrication frame building the belly of his new ship.

"Watch yourself, tough guy," Holly warned, then, as if a light went off over her head, she turned to Lady Amanda.

"Speaking of which...Would you care to comment on Winston's brand new behng-bag of bravado? What did you do to Winston's brain, Doctor? He's sure gotten muy macho since last we met. I'd say it's sexy, but he has the worst timing."

Shame blossomed in deep red on Lady Amanda's face.

Winston froze, then glowered at the doctor. "What does she mean by that?" He took a numb step toward her. His words felt weak in his mouth.

"I had to make some difficult choices, Winston. I'd hoped you would understand in time," Doctor Amanda admitted, backing away.

A cold-water chill trickled down his spine. Now it made sense. His doubts resolved into horrifying clarity and his suspicions proved true. The evidence was all there.

He was shooting guns like an expert marksman, better than most of her guards. As he considered it, he had just beaten up a bunch of skypirates like an action hero with no training in hand-to-hand combat and it came so naturally!

Despite being winded and lacking the physical conditioning for it, his skill was advanced enough to compensate for his poor health. The lifelong fear of having his brain reprogrammed was now reality, igniting a deadly fury more intense than he'd ever felt in his life.

"You behnged with my brain!" Winston roared, flipping a chair out of his way as he approached the noblewoman. "I'm not your lab rat!"

From the corner of his vision, he caught Holly's entertained smirk. Her obvious delight at the depth of his violation made Winston's brain sizzle all the more.

Doctor Amanda had been talking all this while. Words poured out of her but fell on deafened ears, as Winston was in his own inner hell. He swung his focus numbly back in her direction.

"... I needed to keep Quentin safe. He would not stay home like he ought to, so I had to find other options. You needed work, and a new airship. Why not solve all the problems at the same-" she flinched as Winston flipped over a table she had slid behind. "-same time?" she stuttered.

Amanda's eyes grew wide keeping pace with Winston's seething anger. She tried to soothe him with a weak smile. "So I added a few minor, small, little... upgrades?"

Winston felt a subtle change in air-pressure as the office door opened. "A few upgrades?" he growled.

Several arms tried to subdue him with a gang tackle as the guardsmen reacted to the now actualized threat to the Baroness. With some deft moves, Winston slipped their grabs, sending one guardsman into the hanger window glass, shattering it into a white spider web.

"Looks like you amplified his aggression a bit too much," Holly teased Lady Amanda.

He plucked a pair of guardsman stun batons out of their holsters and swept their legs. Winston drove another man face first into a nearby cabinet with a loud crunch and spray of blood. Another attacker he torqued over Lady Amanda's desk and into her office chair, knocking both onto the floor in a tangled heap.

From the corner of his vision, Winston saw Holly bouncing up and down slightly, like a gladiator's girlfriend cheering on his martial display. It annoyed him all the more, but his focus never wavered from Lady Amanda.

Winston stood in the center of a battered heap of Puala'Lolo's best fighters. The skypirates stood back, watching with a 'not my problem' attitude.

"Yep, definitely too much," Holly quipped. "You made yourself one purg of a killer, My Lady! I might want to borrow him sometime."

"Hoss, what're you doin'?" Billy Joe gasped.

Winston whipped around to see his horrified loadmaster staring at the pile of guardsmen he'd just maimed. His blood-spattered hands brought forward the realization of what he had just done.

The remaining rational part of himself agreed with Billy Joe's horror, but the red tinged rage still darkened his mind. A terrified animalistic instinct was in his body's pilot's seat and his rational self was along for the ride.

"I don't understand. They were just small upgrades. They shouldn't have caused such a reaction," Amanda protested, trying to analyze what had gone so wrong, as she cowered in the corner of her office, nowhere left to run.

Winston spun back around and stalked toward her. "A few small upgrades don't do this! You wanted a killer, so you souped me up like one of your mechoids!" Winston shouted, making Amanda flinch.

"I haven't touched your morality or memory! I just added skills you could use, shou-" Amanda pleaded against Winston's emotional torrent.

"You didn't bother to ask!"

Winston gave a crushing back kick to one of the house guards who tried to ambush him from behind, continuing to advance on her.

"Tsk-tsk. Your violation of cyber-ethics aside, you can't amplify emotional response without consequences to morality and decision making. Or so one of my cyberneticists warned me," Holly lectured the terrorized doctor. "It could create a suppressed trigger for psychotic events. In this case, may I present our dear Winston as case in point?"

"Xiao on a cracker, Hoss," Billy Joe breathed.

"And because you had a need, and I was at your mercy, you took advantage of me," Winston hissed. "Mother told you to be my protector and patroness. Paid you well, too!"

"And I have and will be, but now your value is-" Amanda tried to explain.

"I don't give a cheis about what you think my value should be! It's my mind! My life! My decision! For behng's sake, you could have given me the chance to say yes!"

"I didn't have time!" Amanda pleaded as Winston loomed over her.

"We had all the time we needed!" Winston thrust his hand forward to grab her by the throat, desiring to choke the lies out of her.

"Winston, no!" shouted Billy Joe, snaking his coal-black sand arms around his partner, restraining him. "Easy now, Hoss," he soothed into his ear. "This ain't worth killing over, but we're gonna make it right."

Winston screamed in inarticulate frustration, remembering how he couldn't break free the last time Billy Joe caught him in a half-nelson.

"I warned you, Doctor," came a familiar voice from a computer speaker. "You shouldn't have tampered with his mind."

Winston froze in mid-rampage. "Wha-?"

All eyes turned toward the speaker on the floor by Amanda's desk.

"Hello, Winston," Mother said. Her tone was cool and professional. "It seems we have ourselves in quite a fix again, and I need you to calm down enough so we can all survive."

"Well, hello there, Mother!" Holly said, brightly clapping her hands together.

A holoprojector fired up, and Mother's avatar appeared in the room. She regarded Holly for a moment, sighed, then turned her back on the assassin.

"Of course, Dolly survived. Isn't that just grand?" Mother said tartly and manifested a mint julep to sip.

Holly was so dumbstruck, her mouth slapped shut with a tight grimace.

"I could say the same about you, Mother," Winston grunted as he tried to slip free from Billy Joe, but as before, he couldn't break his partner's grasp.

"Don't get lippy with me, young man. We're in a tight spot and need to be smart. Now. Winston, sit down. You, too, Doctor. We're going to work this out like professionals and get everyone what they want so we can all walk away happy…ish. More or less."

16.

Mother's hologram cast her eyes around the room. "Is everyone sitting comfortably?"

Amanda's chair had been put back together, but it wobbled from a cracked wheel. Winston stewed angrily in his seat, while Billy Joe stood protectively over him, ready to restrain his partner. Mother and Holly stood on opposite sides of Amanda's now empty desk, while Quentin kept working on the corner workstation, seeming to have ignored the fight.

After helping up the beaten house guards, the skypirates sat around the edge of the lab on lab tables and stools. They had lightheartedly teased the losers of the fight, treating them like good-natured drunks who fell down in a bar, unsure of how they got there.

No one answered Mother's question.

"Very well, then. Winston, we will have to delay getting to your issues for the moment. Let's assess the situation we're in," she said, as if beginning a board meeting.

"But-" Winston started complaining.

"Later," Mother chided. "This first."

Winston clenched his teeth at the dismissal. His new cognitive implants boiled in a blood red rage that pounded at the inside of his head like an out-of-control roommate trashing the apartment.

Thankfully, Billy Joe standing above him gave his rational mind the strength to deny his desires the power to act. Otherwise, all his psyche wanted to do was cower from the emotional chaos. It was taking everything he had to keep the rage inside.

"What's done is done. We can't address it now," Mother stated, ending further protests.

Winston fell back into a silent pout. His problems were more immediate and possibly faster to cure. Couldn't they see the logic in helping him first?

"My Lord Quentin?" she said. Professor Q perked up at his name. "We're ready for you."

"Yes. Excellent," Quentin said, then looked around the room, blinking in surprise. "My, what a mess. What happened? Oh, nevermind. Nevermind." He picked up a tablet and came over to the desk. There, he fired up another display projector. "It seems we do have an alien species infesting my research library." His voice was a disheartened groan.

"It would be all the more fascinating if it wasn't obliterating centuries, if not millennia, of history as it went. It's a pair of silicon-based lifeforms. This fungus-like creature is the primary species in an alien ecological progression. It breaks down carbon based life and makes it fertile for something else in its ecosystem to live on," Quentin's face hardened as he recited the grim facts.

"We have seen that it's a very aggressive colonizer and might destroy all carbon-based life and organic matter on Puala'Lolo if it escapes into the wild," the professor concluded soberly.

"Dat stuff grows so fast it makes Kudzu look like a brick," a skypirate interjected. This got a glare from Holly.

"That's true," Quentin answered the unsolicited commentator. "And it's tough. More akin to silicone than crystalline silica, although it has some sort of structure to it, and a hardened armored shell that grows over time, from what information I've found so far. In later stages it forms glass-like armor, reinforced with veins of diamondoid from sequestered carbon. In this regard, it becomes like coral."

"This is just peachy, Prof. So we have to kill it like the mold it copies. I hope it burns well. Oh, wait. Fire only makes it grow faster. I dunno where we're going to find a fungicide to kill that stuff," Winston griped. "But what about those things trying to eat our asses?"

"Winston," Mother warned.

"Ah!" Quentin gave a joyful shout. "Those! I found some information in the Imperial Archives.

So fascinating. Very limited, though. Lots of denial of access, so it seems someone doesn't want these creatures to be common knowledge," Quentin added and flipped to some new images. A picture of one of those monsters floated above the desk, but it was much bigger. "This was one bit of video footage an explorer found towards the edge of the known Dream."

Everyone flinched and groaned at the image.

"It's about half the size of one of your gunboats," Quentin said to the skypirate, who voiced his mind earlier.

"Holy Xiao," Amanda breathed. "That's in our research library?"

"Hundreds of them at last check," Billy Joe said.

"The explorer named them 'mycoliths'. They also seem to be a form of silicon-based fungus-like species, and mimic standard carbon-based life as we know it."

"How the purg does it float?" Holly asked.

"The bulbous body is filled with bladders of hydrogen gas that is generated from consuming organic materials," Quentin said.

Questions poured in.

"What's with the iridescent layers on top?"

"How is that antenna acting like a taser?"

"Why is it rocket propelled?"

"Why does this thing even exist?"

"Calm down everyone!" Mother shouted over them all. "Please continue, Lord Quentin."

He nodded toward Mother in thanks. "We know little about their existence, let alone their biology. The plethora of bionic-like systems brings into question whether or not it is an artificial creation. What I have found suggests that this mycolith is the apex predator, and to a certain extent, guardian of a sophisticated ecosystem of silicon-based life. I think they protect the fungus from potential intelligent threats."

"So they're the top and bottom species of a hostile ecology," Amanda supposed.

"What else do you know about this flying purple people eater?" Winston demanded. His dissociated brain allowed him to hear the sullen teenage level disrespect in his voice and it shocked him. A dichotomy had formed in his brain and was granting him a rare level of introspection. Doctor Amanda's artificial warrior implants tried to solve everything with violence, and his own natural instincts wanted to retreat and hide from the pain and fear.

"Being petulant isn't a good look for you, Winston," Mother snapped. "It's time you put on your big boy pants and get with the program like the rest of us."

Winston felt the hot flash of anger followed by a chill in the pit of his stomach at the embarrassment. He'd been so focused on his own violation, he was lashing out. Cognitive dissonance battered his conscience. Now aware of his sullen selfish behavior, his ego put his metaphorical foot down against the programming and reminded himself it wasn't all about him. This crisis was not happening to him, he was just stuck in it like everyone else, the mature, rational part of his mind scolded.

The implants rebelled, throwing more flaming hot accusations against the unassailable logic, but his true self continued gaining strength. Yes, he was a victim of Lady Amanda's neuro-tampering and nothing would change what was done. Mother was right. This awareness gave him the ability to control his reactions and he could work with that.

As Winston's clarity of mind grew, he felt a sense of calm again. He could understand it was a side issue, after all. What was of greater importance was going on around him outside his skull. He was merely a fellow passenger in the middle of another disaster. If he did not pull his head out of his own pucker, he would not survive this.

"Winston?" Mother asked.

"Yoo hoo! You with us, Winston?" Amanda started getting up with that concerned physician look on her face.

Winston looked around the room and saw a bevy of varied expressions ranging from concerned to irritated. Clearly, he'd been doing something that concerned them as he fought in his head.

Winston nodded. "Sorry, having an argument with myself. I'm here. Was I gone long?"

"Long enough," Holly said. Even she had a faint look of concern for him.

"What are we doing?" Winston asked.

Mother sighed. "We're going to have to go back. Probably to where this all started in Secure Reception, with enough firepower to clear out that infestation, save the cases and everything else we can."

"Like Chief Shircan?" Quentin asked.

Mother took control of the holoprojector and started flipping through security camera footage till they stopped in the vaults under the chateau. Camera after camera showed a man watching plugged air vents and the main vault door.

"Seems like these mycolith have them boxed up in there. I hope the chateau has been hermetically sealed," Amanda said.

Mother paused for a moment. "It is now," she said as she locked down every door, vent, drain and window that she could.

"Look. The ventilation system is being used against us. Those things must have eaten the air purifiers. There's no telling if we can ever clean out this stuff!" Quentin groaned.

"Seems to be a reasonable assessment," Mother agreed. "The mycolith have already eaten your internal maintenance drones, and those they didn't get are being dealt with by those inside-out oyster mushrooms." A drone hung from a cascade of those cartoonishly inflated mushroom ears like a fly on a pest strip, slowly being absorbed into the fungus' structure.

"I remember seeing those killer tadpoles eat the fungus, too," Winston said.

"Probably getting the silicon out of those, too. It must be that species' idea of good bio-availability," Amanda suggested.

There was a flash, and the image jumped as a shockwave shook the camera hard.

The view switched to focus on a lab that had just exploded from one of the dying creatures. Several more floated nearby like fish, unconcerned by the death of one of their school. Some of them had developed a second and third diamond on their bellies.

"Why are they exploding like that?" Holly said.

"Circumstantial evidence suggests that these creatures can generate quite high voltages too. That iridescent skin on top of their hydrogen bladders is covered in photovoltaic cells," Quentin said. "Far more powerful than electric eels."

"Greeeeeeaaaat..." moaned one of the skypirates.

"But the hydrogen doesn't explain these extreme explosions we've been having. They're like we lit off dynamite," Winston observed.

"That last one Winston shot in the hangar had a dim blue burst of flame. Hardly an explosion. But when Miss Ho- Lady Nightshade shot it, then it blew up in a huge fireball," Billy Joe reminded Quentin.

"That personality mod's gonna get you in trouble, Bubby," Holly warned as his southern manners came up to the edge of giving her other name away.

"What kind of monstrosity of biochemistry and genetics are these things?" Mother exclaimed. "Xiao must have been playing around somewhere."

"Din't Ygar say something about smelling silane gas?" Billy Joe wondered.

"Who?" Mother demanded.

"A maintenance man over at the...never mind. He smelled it somehow," Quentin said.

"Silane? That would account for the explosions. If these things are generating a related compound, that could explain their rocket propulsion. It's incredibly explosive on contact with air. Instant rocket fuel." Amanda breathed, awestruck.

"And if'n their little diamond storage tanks got cracked... whackaboom!" Billy Joe added.

"Whackaboom indeed," added Amanda. "These things just scream bioengineering."

The camera views flipped through the offices and came upon a data room. It was overflowing with the fungus.

As they watched, one of the banks' sides bulged and fell apart, revealing the grotesque merger of the glass fiber and rare earth elements with growing fungus.

"Guess you and Billy Joe aren't safe after all," Holly sniffed at Mother. "Looks like those things find your guts particularly tasty."

"If they get inside the casing," Billy Joe said.

"Tell me, Crusher," Holly purred maliciously, "how are your systems cooled? One hundred percent sealed system?" Holly said.

"Aw cheis," Billy Joe groaned.

"That's right, you have some air vents too, and these things are probably growing from spores. They'll get inside you and your components, especially your fiber and silicon parts, will get eaten up like spaghetti and meatballs."

Mother looked nervous for the first time. "Holly? Winston? I think it's imperative that you get those cases out of there as fast as possible."

A new camera image of the cryptography lab came up. It was empty save for the creeping fungus. No cases anywhere.

"You said you sent them there?" Mother demanded of Amanda.

"I did. They should be there now," she replied.

"Not stored some place else?" Mother started flipping through cameras. So many were out of commission, covered up and in the process of dissolving or misaligned. Some worked and showed the havoc that the mycoliths had wrought upon the research library's subterranean catacomb of services and labs.

"They shouldn't be," Amanda sounded worried, too.

"Did they get stuck in transit?" Winston offered. "Check the mail-room."

Mother flipped to the cameras there and saw a catastrophe. Racks in the warehouse had tumbled, some smashed into the mailroom at the center of the receiving warehouse, caving in the offices on one side. Fungus piles were growing everywhere. Then the camera image froze as a small school of mycolith fry floated by, randomly attacking each other.

On a tall rack sat the twin cases in the center of the room. A thicket of the fungus climbed toward them from the floor, slowly creeping up the legs. The mailroom equipment was already piles of dissolving electronics.

"Looks like you're in for a penny and a pound if you want those cases, Dolly," Mother snipped.

"Xiao nahq it," Holly growled, turning toward her pirate mates. "All right then, who's up for killing an alien species for fun and excitement?"

There was a dismal groan from the brigands.

"It seems there's a lack of motivation here," Holly said. "I'm fine with your dissatisfaction, as long as you obey."

The skypirates gave long sour stares at the woman they called Lady Nightshade.

"I prefer 'fun and profit' more than what this is," Top protested.

"'Screaming death by alien critter nom-nom'," Dungle muttered.

"Got a way to generate some bix off of this?" Malcolm asked.

"How about it, My Lady?" Holly said, turning to Amanda. "I know she doesn't have any cash right now." Holly gestured to the hologram. "The resurrected rarely do."

"True," Mother conceded to Holly. "I suffer from a liquidity issue only for the moment. This will soon change."

"You brought them here on your own dime," Amanda pointed out. "We would appreciate the help, but don't come to me palm up."

"Besides, sweetheart," Winston said, smirking at Holly's predicament, "You don't pitch in, and you won't have cases left to get. Of course, if the cases do survive, it becomes a finders-keeper's situation."

Holly's lips went from light pink to black and back again in a flash as her withering gaze bounced off Winston's amusement.

"They've got a point," Holly said to the skypirates. "I don't get those cases, the captain doesn't get his share from me, and you won't get your booty."

The skypirates' interest perked up a little more. Winston's shoulders heaved gently in silent laughter. Holly gave him a dirty look.

"Allow me to put a pickle on top of this motivational sundae," Mother chimed in. "Distracted, sullen, half-assed participation in this endeavor against a hungry threat that sees you as nothing more than food will probably get you killed. Everyone needs to drop their own baggage for a little while and pull together. So I think you should consider getting a lot more motivated."

"There is that," muttered Jane.

"Nahq it," said Top. "I hate crypto-critters."

The room fell silent for a while as they made up their minds.

"Does this mean my jolly crew has my back?" Holly asked the skypirates.

This time, their grumble of affirmation grew.

"Whatever doesn't kill you makes you stronger," Quentin cheered the lukewarm response.

"Ever hear of chemical or biological weapons?" Top asked.

Quentin retreated from the rebuke. "Just...just trying to make... bolster people's... nevermind."

"Show some respect to our host," Holly told Top.

"Aye, M'Lady," Top said with a slight dip of respect.

"So, how's we gonna do this?" Billy Joe asked.

"Carefully at first, then probably with extreme violence," Mother said.

Smiles and a rumble of vicious chuckles came from the skypirates.

"I think we've achieved consensus," Holly said.

"At least we know energy and ballistic weapons can kill mycoliths, but we gotta stay clear for when they blow. As for the fungus, we're going to need a miracle," Winston said.

"We'll go over there and free Shircan, and hopefully by then you and the good Doctor will come up with a way to fight the creeping crud."

"And I'm going with you," Quentin announced. The horror on Lady Amanda's face was almost comic.

"No!"

"I have to," Quentin said. "I'm the only one who can get into the vaults that Shircan is in. You can't open them from the inside and Nutty is in no condition to move. There is nobody else."

Winston had no idea where Amanda found the steel for her soul, when she nodded in agreement to his logic

"Good. Then let's get to it," Mother agreed.

Winston turned to Amanda. "If I survive, we're going to have a long talk about what you did to me. Since the damage is done and I have a handle on it for now, I may as well ask."

He cocked an eyebrow. "While you were screwing around in my head against my will, did you upgrade my piloting skills?"

Lady Amanda gave him a mischievous grin.

17.

"Happy to be back in the pilot's seat, Flyboy?" Holly asked Winston as he readied to lift off. The skypirate who was supposed to be at the controls shot dirty looks at the pair from the navigator's seat.

"He ain't," Winston said with a backwards nod of his head toward the pilot behind him.

Winston then executed a tactical dust off. The snappy maneuver overwhelmed the dropship's gravitational dampers, and everyone's stomachs dropped to their feet. Diving out of the cliffside hanger their guts rattled up their spines as Winston leveled off to skim a few feet over the waves. One of the skypirates screamed in joy, another in shock. Blasting out of the hanger, he achieved cruising speed a few seconds later, giving a few jinks and jukes to warm up his reflexes.

"Gunners have a copy?" Winston said into his comm.

A trio of "ayes" came back.

"Are we hot? Remember, the targets we're shooting at can feel your smart sights. So you can't use active locks, or smart targeting. Gonna have to eyeball it as best you can with passive infrared overlays. Copy?" Winston checked, skimming the ocean. A massive rooster tail of water blocked the rearview cameras as he rushed for History Island.

"Rog dat."

"Copy."

"Gotcha."

The airspace above the theme park was clearing out as the Puala'Lolo guardsmen evacuated the tourists. A flock of yachts scattered to the seas from the casino port in the pale gold of the afternoon light. Winston gave them a wide berth and banked higher, swiveling to give the turret gunners the best possible firing solutions.

"We're clear on the point we are to only shoot the mycoliths, nothing more. Right?" Mother's voice came through the comms.

"10-4, Mother. We got this," Winston responded. "Keep working on that way to kill the fungus. It's digging through the ground in places over here."

He took up a position several hundred feet above the research library's cove. The grounds looked mostly undisturbed, except for an occasional tree falling over, and the pearly geysers of fungus in the manicured gardens, spreading as fast as a wildfire, snuffing out the green foliage as it went.

"There's dozens of them critters floating 'round out there," one of the gunners said.

"So? Who's stopping you from shooting?" Winston demanded.

"No one gave the order," the skypirate said, then a hand went over his mic. "Am I supposed to call him 'sir' or something?"

"I don't know. That's why I'm asking you!" a distant voice of another skypirate answered.

"Shoot the behnging things!" Holly yelled into the comms.

"Okay! Okay!" the first skypirate said, startled.

Laser and auto musket fire erupted from the three hardpoints as the turrets tracked the white hot targets floating near the ground. Terrific silane boosted explosions made the ground vomit into the sky. Winston leisurely slid the dropship in a slow strafing run, giving the gunners clean firing lines and backfields.

He marveled at how much combat piloting Doctor Amanda had downloaded into his head. The info flowed naturally into his own skill, enhancing his actions with a nuance to make the gunners more effective.

Quentin came up to the cockpit to watch.

"Get back in your seat, Prof. It's not safe yet," Winston warned.

"But I want to see what's going on! This is so exciting!" Quentin whined. The ground erupted with a huge fireball, way too close for comfort. "Wow!" the Baron gasped.

The shockwave was visible to the naked eye. It swatted the dropship like a newspaper smacking a dog. Jolting the dropship hard enough to overwhelm the grav buffers.

Winston leaned over to face Quentin and bellowed, "Siddown, Prof!" His face red with the shout.

Quentin gave a squawk of fear and rushed back to his seat.

"I must admit, Winston, this is kinda fun," Holly said. Her lips turned an exciting fuchsia, and her eyes washed between iridescent orange then cyan. He squinted curiously at her. Her mood-lips and eyes glitched more, and he realized the unattractive combo was fear leaking out. He permitted himself a smirk at her discomfort.

"Yep. Beats rush hour traffic in Metroballis," Winston agreed.

A dark shape the size of a bloated barracuda rushed up from the ground and slammed into the dropship. With a loud bang, the creature bounced off the pandifico armor plates and readied for another charge.

"What was that?" came Dungle's panicked shout from the rear.

"Uh…I didn't consider this," Winston muttered.

"Consider what?" Holly moaned.

"Surface-to-air monsters. They're rocket propelled, remember?" Winston engaged in evasive maneuvers, climbing to escape the creature's counter attack.

They heard more bangs as other mycoliths kamikazed into the dropship. He ascended faster, giving everyone a disorienting rollercoaster loop. As he went over the top, Winston saw a score or more of the creatures in hot pursuit.

The mycoliths' propulsion was able to keep pace with Winston's evasion, like a swarm of sparrows dive-bombing an owl in flight.

"Shoot the ones coming for us!" Winston yelled into the comms. He tried to dodge the creatures while angling so his gunners had a chance to shoot them.

Two of them exploded nearby, the shockwaves setting off damage alarms, as the dropship reacted poorly to the blasts.

The dropship wallowed in the air like a drunken pelican, twisting and turning as Winston fought to keep from getting hit again. A gap cleared by the gunners appeared and Winston risked flying through it, attempting to regain advantage in this dogfight. The sudden acceleration crushed everyone back into their restraints. Even Billy Joe had to clamp down harder where he stood on the piece of deck.

Winston spotted the seal-sized mycolith zip up in front of him and threw the dropship into a barrel roll. They didn't make it. The sickening creature went through one of the grav fan's intake wells, and instantly compacted to the size of a walnut, which exploded a split second after it spit out the back of the fan, right next to the tail.

Shockwaves shattered several panes of the windscreen, almost tearing it free. The starboard side wing broke off and the *Cavalier Diabolique* fell like a broken-back bird, shot out of the sky by a hunter.

A half dozen voices wailed in terror through Winston's comms. Gravity dampers failed, and the dropship plummeted in a strange flapping manner that looked like it was falling down invisible stairs. The port grav fan tried to regain stability but kept flipping her around.

Winston's hands ached from fighting against the roaring wind to keep hold of the controls. How he wasn't killed by the canopy caving in was a pure miracle. His newly installed skills guided his actions in an effort to stabilize the airship and minimize the inevitable crash.

By the first thousand feet, he isolated out one axis of their tumble. By the second thousand, using the port engine and flaps, he was able to minimize the other two axes and slow their rattling descent.

Winston rolled them over to a still terrifying fifty-degree bank, instead of being upside down. The ground was just seconds away. Metal and pandifico squealed with every twist, ready to tear free. Winston pumped and dropped the throttle on the port engine trying to slow their descent. The altimeter kept ticking down in pulses.

"Brace for impact!" he screamed, then goosed the throttle one last time. Holly's face was paper white. He prayed it would get them below terminal velocity, even if by only a fraction.

It was enough.

The dropship cratered on its belly, hard. It slid backwards in the soft soil of the gardens, digging a short trough, deep enough to scrape the outer structure of the underground facility. It came to a stop in a torn up pile of roses. Its twisted fuselage jutted upwards, rocking slowly, bent into a kinked helix. The port wing stabbed up in the air as if reaching for the sky it had just been thrown out of.

From above, the swarm of victorious mycoliths descended upon their kill.

18..

"Any a y'all left alive?" came Billy Joe's call. All around him was chaos and ruin. Seats had torn from walls with skypirates and guardsmen in them, most injured, some dead. Stripped wires popped like flashbulbs and showered sparks, illuminating the mangled ship's interior in bursts. Streams of light leaked through cracks in the bent fuselage and the loading ramp that dangled in the air snapped off all but one of its hinges. Dirt and flowers had shoved their way into the fuselage through blown seams and missing windows.

"I think I'm dead," Malcolm groaned. "I smell flowers everywhere."

"You died and went to the Purg of Scented Candles," Dungle grunted, as he fought with his harness to release.

"Shut your Boodisht mouth, Dungleberry," Top said.

"Behng you, Top. Keep it up and I'll send you to the Purg of Dental Torture," Dungle fired back.

"You're a really cheisy Boodisht," Jane spat.

"Behng you, too."

"Hoss, you alive up there?" Billy Joe called up front, slowly picking his way through the wreckage. He passed Quentin who remained strapped into his seat, which remained attached to the wall.

Billy Joe checked his pulse and breathing. A knot on the side of his head and one purg of a shiner were forming. He must have hit his head against his crash cage hard, but the Baron was still alive.

There came a familiar moan as Winston came to his senses.

"I'll take that as a yes," Billy Joe said, sliding forward to the cockpit. "Prof's alive too, if you wanted ta know."

"Hurrayyyy," Holly said weakly.

Billy Joe could see the cockpit was half buried in dirt. Broken irrigation pipes were turning it into mud. More soil slurry slid down, entombing them even more.

"Nice landing," Holly fussed while fighting with her mud clogged restraints. "Hey, Bubby. C'mere. Cut me loose. Flyboy isn't quite awake yet," she ordered.

Billy Joe looked out of the canopy's remains to assess how bad their situation was. Somehow, Winston had gotten them to belly land, which had saved their lives, but they were at the bottom of a ten-foot-deep trench.

He reached out, morphed his hand into shears and gently nipped off the harness straps from Winston and pulled his partner from the dirt, his eyes on the sky, watching the mycolith circle.

"Hey!" Holly said. "Whatever happened to 'ladies first'?"

"Two things," Billy Joe said as he set Winston down in a still intact seat. He pointed his shears hand at her. "First, you ain't no lady, and second, he's my partner. He gets priority. And if that ain't enough, he just saved all-a-y'all's lives with this landing."

"Crash landing," Holly grumbled as she tried to pull herself out of the dirt. Billy Joe enjoyed her struggle.

"You do better, next time," he said, and with a snip and a yank, pulled her unceremoniously out of the mud.

A text pinged Billy Joe.

~ ~ ~

MOTHERROAD001: "What went wrong?"

SMLOADMASTER: "I assume this is MOTHERADMIN?"

MOTHERROAD001: "Of course it is! You should change your ID as well."

SMLOADMASTER: "We got shot down by one of those mycoliths. Winston almost got us out of the way, but it was too much for him. Those naqh things are kamikazes as well as cannibals."

MOTHERROAD001: "What's your situation?"

SMLOADMASTER: "Two skypirates and four guardsmen dead so far, most survivors wounded to one degree or another. The rest of us will continue on. We've done a lot of damage to the critter population, but it's not enough."

MOTHERROAD001: "Lady Amanda wants to know if the Baron is all right."

SMLOADMASTER: "He's got a knot on his head and a purg of a black eye, but he is fine. Winston saved our behinds."

MOTHERROAD001: "You're a smoking wreck!"

SMLOADMASTER: "And like I said, Winston saved us. Do you have a way to kill the fungus?"

MOTHERROAD001: "Not yet. Still working on it. She's having difficulty because we don't have any samples to work with and simulations aren't accurate."

MOTHERROAD001: "Can you finish the job?"

SMLOADMASTER: "Unsure. Got no choice now but to try and get the cases with what we got. Exterminating everything is going to require more than what we can do right now."

MOTHERROAD001: "We shall send another airship to pick you up at the landing pad. Good luck and don't get killed."

SMLOADMASTER: "Roger that."

~ ~ ~

"Get off there, you!" came a shout from outside, followed by the roaring hiss of a fire extinguisher, then came cackling laughter. "Go on! Git!"

Billy Joe looked up towards the source of the voice, bewildered. Other survivors were doing the same. Then a few more blasts of the extinguisher were heard, mixed with the buzzing of drones, hissing spray, more human yells and little alien shrieks. Then all went silent. A few tense moments later, a low, self-satisfied chuckle drifted down.

Billy Joe slid up toward the sound just in time for a hand to slap the side of the crumpled, but still closed, hatch.

"Any y'all alive in there?" came a voice.

"Ygar?" Billy Joe said, surprised.

"Yeah." the handyman answered. "Y'all wrecked yer jet. Don't think I can fix 'at, though."

"That's okay, Ygar," Billy Joe called. "Stand back. I'm gonna tear the hatch off. We gotta get outta here."

"I got the tractor here an' a big hunk a chain," Ygar offered.

"No need. I got this," Billy Joe said.

The mechoid took hold of the deck with his leg skirt and braced while he slid his nanite arms into the cracks of the jammed door. He expanded them like the jaws of life, and the hatch crumpled with ease. With a quick jerk, he dislodged the door from the frame.

About ten feet up from the fuselage hatchway, there stood Ygar, bracketed by mounds of thoroughly obliterated flower beds and decorative ferns. It took Billy Joe a few moments to comprehend what he saw in the background. With his long nanosand tendrils, he winched himself up the side of the trench to stand with the handyman. The surrounding conflict left him amazed.

Dozens of groundskeeping drones buzzed about with fertilizer tanks, spraying the fungus, which promptly became rusty looking, then devolved rapidly to an ugly festering umber.

"What the purg have you done?" Billy Joe exclaimed as he watched a pest control drone chasing a bluegill sized mycolith like a cartoon cat and mouse. The drone squirted liquid at it as it chased the creature before vanishing around the other side of the wrecked dropship. The mycolith's shrieks of terror faded.

"Done what now?" Ygar asked.

"How are you killing that stuff?" Billy Joe asked, pointing at the silicone fungus.

"T'weren't nothin special. It looked like caulking in a bathtub so I squirted it with some grout solvent. Stuff just shriveled up and died. It's comin' out everywhere, so I put it in landscaping sprayers and hosed 'em down like I was killing weeds. Works on them molds real quick-like. Them sky fishes though, don't like it none too much. It won't kill em, but they run like cats from a water bottle." Ygar laughed as another pair zipped by in a bizarre dogfight.

"Got em runnin' all over the island like that!" He howled with laughter as a drone chased after another small mycolith. Winston crawled out of the hatch. Billy Joe turned to lend his partner a hand. "How you feelin', Hoss?" he asked, lifting him out of the pit.

"Rough," Winston said, brushing lumps of dirt off his mud soaked flight suit.

"What was that 'whooshing' sound I heard?" Billy Joe asked as he reached down to grab hold of Quentin and pull him up like he was on a swing. The professor held a cold pack to his head.

"Fire extinguisher," Ygar said. As he saw Quentin, the handyman gave a little bow. "Why they got you here, M'Lord? This ain't no place for you'un," he said.

"We've got to get in the vault and free Chief Shircan. They need me for that," Quentin said through a wince.

"Why d'you got that fire extinguisher?" Winston asked, pointing to the bright red cylinder the handyman held.

"Oh, they don't like this neither," Ygar said, hefting it up in his arms. The endothermic extinguishers can freeze 'em solid. Makes em easy to dispose of before they explode. Cold keeps Silane gas stable. It'll blow up on its own if'n it gets warm. Plus freezin' these li'l buggers keeps them from releasing the gas into the air."

"What?" Quentin's eyes popped wide open.

"They don't like cold?" Billy Joe said over his shoulder as he hauled Holly out of the wreck.

"Don't like freezing to death none. Seems they go dormant if they get too cold," Ygar said with a shrug, then reached into the bucket on his tractor. "Get em long enough and you get fish sticks that'll blow up in about half an hour or so, depending how frozen they get 'em."

Ygar tossed the trout sized mycolith on the ground before them. Everyone flinched back from the icy carcass. "Got about half an hour before that 'un goes bang. So take a quick look and I'll get it some place safe."

"That thing looks like it should be mounted above a fireplace mantle in a haunted house," Dungle said.

"Prof," Winston said, turning to Quentin. "What's the fire suppression system like in there?"

"I've no idea," Quentin said. "Something that won't harm the antiquities."

"Y'got halon systems in the chateau and some of the labs, but the service areas all have endothermic foam. The sprayed liquid reacts an' draws the heat out of a fire while it foams up 'an smothers the rest. Looks like snow tha's attracted to fire. Relatively harmless once it's done reactin'. Don't get it on yer skin though while it's live. It can give you nasty frostbite in seconds," Ygar explained. "That halon will suck the oxygen right out of yer lungs, though. Thas how it snuffs the fire, but won't wreck electronics."

Winston clicked his comm. It was as dead as the dropship.

"Holly? Try to comm Mother and ask her if she can activate the fire fighting equipment, and let her know about Ygar's grout solvent solution. We need to get more of those groundskeeping drones over here. I think we may be able to turn the tide here."

19..

Winston struggled against his implanted warrior aggression at the slow crawl of their progress. It had been slow going to get into the service corridors under the garden. Dead mycolith blasts had blown holes in the walls and ruptured ceilings at places, letting dirt and sand pour in from above.

Thanks to a fleet of pesticide drones leading their way, fogging down everything with silicone solvent, the fungus was blackened and dying. It fizzed and bubbled before falling apart in hunks and sheets, making wet, messy splats on the floor. If a mask seal gapped even the slightest amount, the chemical smell leaked around the edges with an acrid bite mixed with an unholy rot.

"All right, you're sure you, Professor Q and Ygar, can get to the vaults?" Winston asked as they got to the T intersection to the chateau's vaults.

"Easy," the sergeant responded, his voice muffled by his air mask.

"Rooihemp will be excellent protection, and with Ygar's knowledge of the drones, I don't foresee a problem. Besides, once we get there, Chief Shircan and his men will be more than enough protection," Quentin added.

"Okay, then," Winston said reluctantly.

"Are you sure this plan will work?" Holly asked. "I mean, we're fighting monsters with fire hoses here."

"I saw a movie like that once," Winston said with a cheese-eating smile. "Worked for them, but only after most of the Earth died."

"Oh, joy. That's reassuring," said Dungle.

"Shut up, red shirt," Holly snapped.

"Can we get a move on?" Malcolm demanded. "This air mask is itchy and stupid, and standing still too long could give that crap a chance to grow on us."

"Zip it!" Winston reinforced. "Okay, Quentin. Be careful and run if you have any trouble."

"I'll git him movin' if he goofs around too long," Ygar added with his gap-toothed smile. "Come on, M'Lord."

The Baron, sergeant and handyman, flanked by a quartet of drones before and behind them, walked into the dark hallway to free Chief Shircan and his security detail.

Winston looked at Billy Joe who carried almost two hundred gallons of endothermic firefighting liquid on his back.

"You all set?" Winston asked.

"Like a hound with a fox's scent in my nose," Billy Joe said, his smile still crooked from the wounds he took from their first encounter with exploding mycoliths.

Holly carried a length of hose over each shoulder, while the last four skypirates that weren't too wounded or dead from their crash, had single lengths and a fire extinguisher. A quintet of drones hovered around them, waiting for orders.

"Right, then. The drones will clear the way of fungus. When we get to the receiving warehouse, they'll cut a path into the mailroom, giving us a place to work. Use the fire extinguishers till we can hook the hoses up to the standpipes and maybe we can freeze out all the critters there. Hopefully, we can reach Secure Reception and end the threat for good," Winston repeated the plan as they started making their way down the hall.

The drones pushed ahead, each carrying a five gallon tank and sprayer, while small nanofabricators on top of them refilled them constantly. The solvent spray was so thick it was like walking in fog. Occasionally a little mycolith tried to charge but was driven back by the cloud that led their way down the corridor.

"Why don't we just let the drones do this?" Holly griped.

"They're too dumb," Winston reminded her. We need them frozen so we can dispose of them safely."

Holly let out a groan like a petulant teenager. "Fine!"

Winston loved watching her cool exterior crumble. After so many times of seeing her handle crazy circumstances, with ease, it was a delight to watch her sweat. Her time with the pirates must not have gone so smoothly after all.

Ahead, dim light came out of a sizable hole where the doors to the mailroom used to be.

"I guess that's where that seal sized bastard came out," Jane said. "No way it coulda come through a vent."

"Probably. Billy Joe, you got comms at all?" Winston asked.

"Nope. Too many signal repeaters are down. We're on our own. Best Mother can do is watch and make some good guesses on how to help," Billy Joe said.

"I don't see a stand pipe out here, so hopefully it's just on the inside of the warehouse doorway," Winston said.

"Okay, minor change in plan. First the drones, then Billy Joe. Once he has secured the standpipe beachhead, we come in and freeze whatever's left."

Everyone nodded, satisfied, except for Billy Joe.

"I love how you assume I'm expendable because I'm a mechoid," he complained "I'm scared cheisless too, y'know."

"Sorry, Bubby," Winston proffered.

Just outside the illumination of their lights, dozens, if not hundreds, of pairs of beady little fish-eyes stared at them. Their owners snarling.

"Wow," Jane said in a low voice. "I've been demoted to fish food."

"Then I guess you better win," Holly said.

"Remember, no guns, only cold or solvent," Winston said, and took a deep breath.

"Drones, go!" he ordered, and the five shot into the room letting out full saturation sprays.

More tiny screams of rage echoed in the warehouse as the mycolith fry ran from the cloud of solvent. The faint sizzle built as the chemical began killing the fungus. In the service corridor, the eyes crept a little closer. Top let out a quick blast of his fire extinguisher, and the encroaching monsters moved back. They had learned to respect the cold.

A giant roar of pain and fury vibrated the walls. Bright bluish white light followed with a rumbling gush that reminded Winston of an old rocket launch, and dingy yellow light flickers lit the corridors as debris and chemicals burned. Swarms of mycolith were building up on either side of them. The thick swarms pushed them closer to the warehouse doors.

"Bubby!" Winston shouted, motioning for his partner to lead the way.

Billy Joe let out an auto tuned rebel yell and charged inside. The cry instantly turned into an "Oh, cheis!"

Top sprayed another mycolith as it came in too close. This time, it backed up for only a second or two, the rest closed in like walls of teeth and flickering electric arcs.

"This is coming apart, fast," Holly said. "Behng it. Everyone in!"

"Works for me," Winston said, and they all rushed inside, fire extinguishers blasting away at anything too close.

A frost covered Billy Joe as he held his ground only a few dozen feet ahead, spraying like crazy with his endothermic liquid tanks. A dozen or more flash frozen mycolith fry falling around his leg skirt. "Behnging Xiao!" he shouted. "It's huge!"

The warehouse was lit by hydrogen boosted burning wreckage. Two exploded drones threw up thick black smoke and more smokey yellow orange flames.

There was a thunderous rocketing sound, then a crash. A rack collapsed like a house of cards. The gargantuan shadow of what tumbled it rippled along the walls.

"What's huge?" Top demanded.

"The mama mycolith!" Billy Joe's amplified voice echoed back.

"How big?" Top shouted back.

"Worry about that later! Where's the behnging standpipe?" Malcolm yelled as he pulled pieces of garbage and rubble away from the wall, following the traditional crimson paint.

"Try over there," Winston said, pointing away from the menacing shadow creeping around the back side of the warehouse.

"You, go over there!" shouted Dungle as he saw the mycolith filling in that area. "I'm not becoming fish-cheis!"

"Coward!" Billy Joe growled and backed away from the area he had cleared.

Winston saw even more frozen mycoliths in the debris. "Hoss, this was a brilliant plan, but now we got little fish grenades fallin' out of the skies, putting us in a minefield. Don't know when they's gonna blow, but we best do what we gotta, and quick."

He turned his sprayers around toward the direction of where a standpipe should be and started hosing down the area, driving back the nasty purgspawn as it got too close to Top and Jane. They hollered pain filled epithets at Billy Joe when small spatters of the endothermic chemicals hit their coveralls. Frost, steam and more mycolith fry fell to the ground and smashed like they were dipped in liquid nitrogen. The little tadpole size ones gave off loud cherry bomb bangs.

Winston realized Holly was no longer with them. His eyes scanned around the warehouse to see where she had gotten to.

"Got a standpipe here!" Dungle hollered. Billy Joe rushed to the skypirate and got a hose operating.

"Holly!" Winston called. No answer came back, but he glimpsed her running through the piles of dead fungus and toppled racks, bounding toward the mail-room like an impala on a savanna.

"Nahq it!" Winston exploded and ran after her.

A blast of cold air washed over him from behind as Billy Joe and Dungle got the first hose working. Frost hung in the air and clung to his sweaty body as snow started falling.

Winston's feet constantly tangled in the shattered pallets and wobbling piles of boxes of unknown items as he fought his way toward the mailroom. With increasing regularity, he sprayed mycoliths that started an attack run on him and they fell frozen to the ground.

There was another thunderous rocket blast of blue-white flame and a splash of an exploding drone. Rounding the corner in the dim yellow light of burning solvent, Winston saw the queen mother mycolith. It was so close he could feel heat emanating from its radiator-like fins.

It was the size of a gunboat, easily six yards long, and apparently breathed fire. He gaped, goggle-eyed at the creature. Big lobster claws tore apart crates and boxes, shoveling them into its maw. It swam in the air like a whale, with pops and sizzles of microscopic bursts of silane gas burning like maneuvering thrusters from pores in a large hollow under the monster's stubby rudder-like tail. Diamondoid crystals covered its body, armoring it on all sides, while its belly revealed a cluster of enormous diamonds. The monster gave off a dim flickering rainbow of light from its glass flight fins and crystalline protrusions.

There was no way Winston's little fire extinguisher could stop this thing, or even slow it down. Another drone got too close. In a flash, the mycolith's claw snapped it out of the air. Solvent splashed all over, but the mycolith's armor was immune. It threw the destroyed drone away as it continued to feed. The horror's mouth looked like a garbage compactor had had a baby with an industrial shredder.

A loud whistle caught Winston's attention. Both he and the mycolith turned to look toward the sound.

There Holly stood, illuminated by the room's remaining functional fluorescent lights. Her cases held high above her head in triumph.

"Got what I need, Flyboy! Don't worry, I set the hoses up for you on the center standpipe, but it's time to take what's mine and go! See you another time... if you live!" she shouted and blew him a kiss before disappearing behind some untoppled racks.

Mama mycolith bobbed up and down, confused as Holly vanished behind the wreckage. Winston heard the creature's confused burble and froze when he realized he was but a few yards away from the flying abomination. If it noticed him, he had no place to escape.

When Holly popped out from the devastation again, she'd almost made it to the exit. The mycolith, like an irritated bull, rocketed after her with a deep rumbling growl. Storage racks blocking its path blew apart as the monster charged after her like a plow. Winston slapped his hands over his ears from the calamitous racket. Loaded scaffolds tumbled to the ground crushing everything beneath. Several enormous explosions erupted where mycoliths got caught in the destruction.

The ground jumped as Mama slammed into the warehouse wall, collapsing part of it. The massive beast raged against the barrier, which meant Holly probably escaped, Winston thought. Teeth scraped fibercrete from the wall like a shredder. As he watched, it dawned on him that maybe the monster was trapped! It couldn't bite the weave of girders that turned the warehouse into its cage.

A dog-sized mycolith charged the distracted Winston. At the last second, he caught sight of the movement and put his fire extinguisher up to intercept the sack of teeth that made up the mycolith's mouth. The impact catapulted him back over a dozen feet where he landed in a heap of scrap.

The nasty brute bit down on the half empty fire extinguisher, shaking it like a terrier with a rat. With a squeal of distorting pandifico, it ruptured with a hollow bang, flash-freezing the monster. The explosion hit Winston with a frigid blast, freezing his clothes to the ground where he lay. He could feel the sting of frostbite on his thighs and shins. He howled at the pain.

After a few seconds, the agony ebbed enough for him to move. Things were getting worse all around them, and fast. Explosions from Billy Joe's initial frozen victims started going off like mortar rounds as the dead mycolith thawed out just enough to react with air. Shrapnel whizzed by, ricocheting off the chilled debris.

Holly was gone with the cases. That left them with only the mycoliths to stop. Were they contained enough in here that they could destroy them all with one act?

He heard some more loud thuds and then a terrific grinding of pandifico being chewed by giant mycolith teeth. If that thing got out, he realized, it could be all over for Puala'Lolo. How to stop something so big, and so fast?

Snow started falling all around him as he heard triumphant screaming from the skypirates accompanied by Billy Joe's rebel yell. Winston shoved over one of the piles of old boxes. Mama mycolith was moving around toward them like a malevolent blimp.

It looked like there was an approaching snowblower coming toward him as Billy Joe led the advance toward the mailroom. Drifts and slides of the off-white powder filled in the warehouse on either side, getting closer and closer to the central mailroom.

Winston could see the five of them through the thick sprays, all turned into vague figures slouching through the curtains of fluffy, frozen fire retardant, clearly thankful for their insulated coveralls.

With a shout of encouragement, Winston hustled his way through the chaos of the warehouse and reached the mailroom. Dying fungus proved the drones had done their job, and Holly had hooked up the two hoses to the standpipe next to the fire board. Outside the shattered windows, the snow stopped falling with a series of warning screams.

Behind Billy Joe, the giant mycolith had the hose in its claw and gave a hard yank. Dungle slammed to the floor, but Top and Jane had wrapped the excess hose around themselves. In a flash, they disappeared into the monster's maw that had severed the hose. It bellowed in pain as some of the endothermic foam got inside.

"No!" screamed Malcolm. The skypirate drew his pistol and opened fire. The lasers refracted harmlessly on the diamondoid hide creating more little fires with the fragmented blasts.

"Don't!" Dungle's shout vanished in the roar of the accelerating monster. Winston turned his hose on full blast, hoping to make it turn, but his spray went wild as he staggered under the power of the flow. Malcolm hit the mouth like a fastball hitting a catcher's mitt. The mycolith didn't even slow as it flew through the area where he stood. Billy Joe threw himself out of the way of the low-flying horror. Although it didn't swallow him, the mycolith's bulk smacked him into a debris field somewhere in the dark. Ice burst out on the flank of the monstrosity as Winston finally hit his target.

Its screams were nightmarish as the creature flew out of range and into the dark where the tattered remains of the warehouse helped hide it. The monster was just too big to saturate enough for freezing.

"Bubby!" Winston shouted and stopped spraying to listen for a reply. His hands were numb again. That's gotta be first or second degree frostbite, he thought to himself.

"I'm a'comin!" his partner yelled back. "Just gotta get this rack off me first."

A twenty foot tall section of tangled struts had toppled over and Billy Joe stood up from the mess.

The original fires sputtered out, and it grew darker and colder. Shadows of the mycolith looped around Winston a few times, waiting for its moment. Hiding farther back, he saw human motion.

"Anyone still alive, get over here!" Winston commanded. Dungle, the lone surviving skypirate, obeyed and ran to Winston as fast as he was able and gave another short stream at a mycolith. Most of the smaller creatures were frozen or dead from their primary assault. That left only the big one and whatever remained by the egg pile in Secure Reception.

The beast dove from where it had been hovering near the ceiling. Its rocket-like thrust accelerating it like a missile, mouth wide to gulp down Billy Joe and the skypirate as they ran for the mailroom.

Winston dropped the hose and hit the deck as the mycolith blew through the mail room like a runaway train, scooping out a trench and shearing off the top of the elevator in the center that went down to Secure Reception.

The fire alarm went off.

Dungle and Billy Joe helped Winston to his feet. "Now the alarm sounds?" he griped.

"That's a mechanical warning," Dungle said. "The monster clipped the fireboard and activated the sprinklers. We need to get out now."

"If it's that gas, we can run for the door or sit tight. The masks will protect us, but the halls are gonna be crawling with nasty critters still," Billy Joe observed.

"... But if it's endothermic foam, we'll freeze," Winston agreed, looking at his whitened hands.

"Can't stay in here. Look what it just did, taking a huge swipe outta this little shack. What're we going to do?" Dungle wailed.

Winston looked up to see the mycolith rounding for another dive.

"You got any left in your tank?" Winston asked Billy Joe, gesturing with his curled up hand at his firefighting backpack.

"Enough for a quick fight," Billy Joe agreed.

"Then down the hatch," Winston said, nodding toward the open elevator shaft.

"Geronimo!" Billy Joe shouted and dove into the open elevator.

"Wait, what?" Dungle shouted, as Winston jerked him along, locked together at the elbow.

"Two to catch!" Winston shouted and over the lip they went.

Dungle screamed as they dropped into the dark void as the air became white with frost.

20..

Classical Swing Hop echoed through the street cafes from the club next door, spilling out of the open windows. Holly was relieved it wasn't Electro-Zydeco. That sound made her teeth itch. Her small metal table was a quaint toss back to Parisian chic, where she sipped an Americano and nibbled a few chocolate mini-eclairs as the crowd walked past. Of course, the crowd was on Nova Tortuga, and they were not the touristy sort you'd expect in a place like this. It gave her the image of a mercenary biker gang being forced to have high tea with royalty. They got the concept, but their natural character leaked out around the sides nonetheless.

The client was late for the handoff, according to her internal clock, but only fashionably so. Delayed handoffs were always aggravating, but this was the nature of the beast. Leave too early, the client accuses you of not showing and things get complex. Leave too late, and you may go home with the law, or explode. That was possible, too. But bombs are typically on timers. The fact she wasn't dead already felt like a net positive. Besides, if they did not make the exchange, what was she going to do with these cases?

She popped another mini eclair in her mouth and chased it with another sip of coffee. The remaining two pastries stared up at her as longingly as some of the lonely-hearted men who lacked the courage to approach her. Her sarong was over transparent-as-glass smartex armor that made her skin glisten like she was slicked in suntan oil. Not as good as her typical armor, but would do the job most times. Those who were aware could see the threat. It showed she wasn't an easy mark. All others saw no deeper than the beautiful surface. When the two remaining morsels were gone, she told herself, I'll leave and then figure out what to do next.

"What's a girl like you doing in a nice place like this?" a familiar voice said behind her. She stopped in mid-chew.

"I'm stunned you're here," she said, swallowing hard and wiping her lips with a napkin. "Winston."

He sat down next to her, like two old friends. His arms and fingers wrapped in bandages. The tip of his nose was dark with frostbite, with a multitude of scratches and bruises on his flesh, like he'd just survived a plane crash. She smiled at him casually.

"Good way to get killed, showing up for this meeting, Flyboy." Holly cranked up her limbic manipulator for the nickname she hung on him.

"Not this time, Sweetheart." He tapped two audio filters snugged in his ears like hearing aids. "Not messing with my head sub-sonically this time."

She squinted at him with severe irritation. "Why are you here? And why shouldn't I kill you now?"

"Public venue, lots of witnesses. Commodore Roberts won't be pleased if you do, either. He knows I'm here on business. He likes me," Winston rattled off. His bright Hawaiian shirt, panama hat and khaki shorts made him look like some sort of tourist, but his heavy boots gave the game away. She could see he was unarmed, even without the use of any sensors.

"Of course, the best reason not to kill me is that you want to get paid and be clear of this job, right?" Winston smiled as the thumb screws of money squeezed Holly's greed.

"My client hired you to be his errand boy?" Holly was genuinely shocked. "And you said yes? Clearly you knew it was me who you were seeing."

"Yes, yes, and that's why I said 'yes and yes'," Winston was still smiling that insufferable grin. "I knew you missed me."

His voice was absolute syrup, and she hated him for it. He had the power, and he knew it.

Holly sat in silence, popped another pastry in her mouth and chewed with a purpose. Her eyes scanned all around. And what do you know? There was Billy Joe in the subway station across the street back in the arcade, observing two retired pirates play dominoes and drink out of paper bags.

"And Crusher's your backup," she said with a sneer.

"He refused to be left at home," Winston said. He reclined in his chair, arm propped up on the backrest and looked around like he was just enjoying the sights. "You done being confounded yet?"

"I…" Holly's response died in her mouth as she saw Dungle sitting at the clam bar next door. How did they all slip up on her like this? He raised a glass of chelada beer and squeezed the lime in.

"Trust me, Sweetheart," Winston said, clasping her hand like an old dumped boyfriend trying to get one more night. She wanted to recoil from his warm bandage-covered hands, but couldn't move. "You're surrounded."

Winston looked over his shoulder at Dungle and nodded. "He's none too happy about you, either. Didn't enjoy being left to die like Malcolm, Jane and Top. Little resentful." Winston was toying with her and it was taking all her strength to not fold him in half and kick the package over the next building.

"How did you ever survive, darling," she purred, turning on all her charm, forcing herself to stroke Winston's hands seductively.

"We jumped down the elevator shaft and the fire suppression system did what the hoses couldn't. Froze the nahqed thing into a block of ice. Took them a few hours to get us out. Billy Joe caught us so we didn't go splat, and apparently all the brood went out the air-vents by the time we got in there again, so we were safe," Winston explained.

"You do lead a charmed life," she picked his hand up and raised it to her lips.

"Ah ah ah..." Winston warned and took his hands out of hers. "I don't mind that sexy transparent smartex armor touching me, but no skin to skin contact. Otherwise, Billy Joe will squeeze the juice out of you. We promised Dungle he could shoot your remains and desecrate your body. He's a bit of a sicko."

Holly gritted her teeth. "Verification phrase?" she said, far too sweetly.

"Truth can only exist outside of Xiao. But Xiao is everywhere. Therefore, there can be no truth," Winston sang as a psalter. His voice was definitely not meant for singing, but it wasn't intolerable. Holly winced worse than his performance deserved, but that was because he gave the correct verification. He was her contact.

"When did you become my contact?"

"None of your business," Winston said coldly. Not even a smirk.

In her head, Holly went over all that they'd been through. Was this nobody of a skytrucker a plant? Did he fake so much of this infirmity and weakness? Did he allow her to beat him? There were hints he was smarter and more dangerous than he was. She definitely liked the take charge kung fu fighter pilot expert persona he displayed on Puala'Lolo, but maybe that was all part of some elaborate cover.

Agitated, she popped the final eclair into her mouth and slammed the last of her coffee.

"You're right. It's none of my business," she said, standing up. Full action mode now. "Let's finish this and get you the behng out of my life."

"My sentiments exactly. After you," Winston said, joining her.

She strode across the street with a purpose, Winston close behind. They entered a subway station arcade and walked to an alcove of lockers. There, she paused. Billy Joe waited, reading posters on the walls. Close enough that she could get off a fatal blow on Winston, but Billy Joe would be on her before she could escape. Thwarted by mutually assured destruction.

And then there was Dungle to think about. No doubt Captain Dapper Don MacGee had more skypirates mixed in with the potpourri of Nova Tortuga's daytime population if he was involved.

And since she screwed him out of his last cut, there was hardly a doubt he had more people around.

She held out her hand to Winston like a bellhop asking for a tip. So he copied her. "You may think I'm stupid enough to fork the payment over without even seeing them?"

She smirked at him. "I took a shot. So what? Xiao!" After a brief pause and glare, "You are so amateur hour!" she hissed like an irritated teenage girl.

"Sticks and stones. Can we get over this playground crap? Now I get why I was asked to do this job. You just can't be professional around me anymore. It's always personal and emotional with you," Winston criticized.

"Wha-?" Holly's mouth dropped wide. How dare he! She slid her fingers between the two rows of lockers, grabbed a little string, and pulled a key out that was tied to it. She snapped it off and dangled it between her thumb and index finger in front of him.

"This what you want?" she said, her jaw so tight it hurt.

"If that's where the cases are," he replied.

Winston raised an empty palm again, held it there for a moment, then snapped it closed like he was catching a fly. When his fingers opened again, there was a key there, just like hers.

Holly looked over at Billy Joe, who actively ignored her.

"Okay, I admit that was pretty cool," Holly said and held out her other hand while holding up the key as if to drop it. "Trade on three?"

Winston copied her again. "One," he said.

"Two," Holly continued.

"Three," the pair said in unison, and dropped the keys into each other's hands.

Winston looked at the key for a moment, then chuckled.

"What's so funny?" Holly demanded.

"You'll see. Go to the locker."

The pair walked down the same row of lockers. Billy Joe moved to the end of the row and blocked it off. Nobody would get too curious with him there, Holly observed. They stopped and she realized their keys were directly opposite each other. Holly rolled her eyes as Winston chuckled.

"How're you having fun with this?" Holly growled.

"Because this was a total accident," Winston admitted. "I picked at random."

Holly's fingers were barely able to get the key in the lock. He must be messing with me, she screamed internally.

"Shall we turn on three?" Winston mocked. He must be mocking her!

She gave a grunt of anger and opened her locker. Inside, just as promised, was a data stick and a piece of paper. She heard Winston open his locker and there were the cases as promised.

"I'd love to say this has been a pleasure," Winston said with a grunt, as he lifted the cases out of the locker. "But, it wasn't." Winston snipped.

She boiled and smoked inside at his mockery. His purposefully controlled expression drove her mad.

Holly's mouth opened and closed, until a single syllable, "Yeah," dribbled out.

Winston drew a deep sigh and walked away. She stared after him a long time, even after he was out of sight. Slowly, she opened the piece of folded paper.

"See Dungle," were the only words on it.

"Of course," Holly whispered, crumpling up the paper and throwing it into the trash.

She walked to a bodega further down the arcade to a bank terminal to check the balance.

"Well, what do you know?" she said. "He was legit." The entire payment was on the drive. With a few deft moves, she transferred the money into several accounts and a last memory stick.

Once completed, Holly walked to the clam bar where Dungle was drinking another beer out of a bucket.

"Lady Nightshade," he said as she came close enough to talk.

"What?" she snapped

"You've been very naughty. Captain MacGee is quite cross with you," Dungle scolded.

This day was just getting more and more humiliating, Holly thought when an enormous shadow fell across the bar. Holly turned to see the Amazonian hulk of the First Mate Gaffinger on her rear oblique flank.

"That's right, Nightshade. Cap'n sez yer fate is mine, unless'n ye turn over what be owed?" Gaffinger said. Her posture and tone screamed that she hoped she couldn't pay.

"Is there ever a day you get sick of affecting that silly speech pattern?" Holly snipped.

"I think it's your lucky day, Gaff," Dungle said, verbally licking his chops.

"You're both wrong. Here," Holly said and slapped the data thumb on the bar. "Xiao behng the both of you poxy bastards. I gave the good captain a tip for his trouble. Have to admit I'm surprised you found me here."

"Next time, don't steal a civilian flier with a tracking beacon," Gaffinger said, taking the data stick off the bar with surly disappointment.

"Ah, Lady Junker ratted me out. After all I did for her and her halfwit brother," Holly said. "We square?"

"Almost," Dungle said with a laugh. "Gaffinger, if you'd do the honors?"

Holly braced for an attack, but found only a tri-folded piece of paper in front of her face. "This is the second time someone's handed me paper I didn't want," she said taking the paper from Gaffinger, opening it.

"By order of Commodore D. P. Roberts, you are hereby marooned on Nova Tortuga. Forbidden to leave the skyland on any vessel till he deems you have learned your lesson to not toy with the lives of your betters," Gaffinger said.

Dungle cackled with glee. "If you have any more questions, you can go see the Commodore, if he'll take your audience!"

"If this data thumb be false, we savvy where ye be," Gaffinger said and slapped Dungle on the shoulder. "Shove off," she ordered.

Holly sighed as the pair of skypirates walked down the street. As they disappeared into the crowd, she reached over and took the last remaining beer in Dungle's bucket, flipped off the top, and slammed it down.

"There are worse skylands to be marooned on."

\#   \#   \#

INTERLUDE: JACKPOT IN EVERY SENSE

Despite it being a bittersweet trip, the reincarnated *Sierra Madre* had performed flawlessly on her shakedown cruise. Winston felt like a guilty widower, having lost his childhood sweetheart and first love, coming back from his honeymoon after remarrying a beautiful pinup model who had just shown him all she could do. All her quirks or pet peeves were still unfamiliar and frustrating, but her plentiful charms thrilled him. It would take a lot of time to get used to his new airship.

He'd rechristened her as the "*Maltese Queen*" at a brief ceremony on Puala'Lolo. Lady Amanda insisted they do things right, so he stammered through a short speech then smashed a bottle of nice champagne on the ship's bow, right on her nose art – a stylized representation of his wife, Valerie, as a warrior queen riding a giant peregrine falcon.

His ship wasn't a tug any longer. Instead, she was reborn as a small packet freighter and that meant his career as a skytrucker was over. He was beginning anew as an airship captain. Her flattened-bullet shape mixed with sleek art déco inspired control surfaces made her mega-sonic body the sexiest ship he'd ever had his fingers on.

A luxurious crew and passenger deck came forward from the dorsal engine section, above her double ended cargo bay. Lady Amanda spared no expense there, making sure they all had sumptuous quarters made for courtiers, including drone servants and deluxe food fabricators. Winston supposed she wanted a yacht for when she joined them. A bevvy of multipurpose spaces sat between them and the reactors and gave the impression she or the Baron had plans for them. The Queen's belly was wide enough to carry two side-by-side rows of two containers internally. This cost the airship towing capability, leaving her two small pairs of tractor beams, front and back, only big enough to load containers and cargo. Billy Joe even had a sizeable nanofab workstation able to make a small contingent of service, maintenance and loading drones he could boss around.

Her trio of mini-reactors powered three robust grav jets clustered near the tail in a triangular arrangement. The bottom two snugged up against the rear loading ramp. Although they lacked the same maneuverability as her previous incarnation, she outclassed nearly every commercial vessel in the Dream in terms of speed. Mach-19 was as high as Winston risked testing her long legs on this run, but she could probably go 15-20 percent faster if he had to. It might even be possible for the Queen to escape from imperial cruisers and dreadnoughts. Fighters and gunboats had little chance of catching her. Though anyone who picked on her was in for a rude surprise. She packed enough firepower in her camouflaged weapons pods to regret their choices if they lived.

The runtime to Nova Tortuga took about a third of what it normally would and good weather had made the return trip to Puala'Lolo even faster. She slid effortlessly into the local atmosphere. It was strange to feel like he was home again.

Winston chatted with local ground control for his flight path back to the compound. It looked like a great day for a swim, he thought as he slowed on his approach, the cliff-side entrance to land in the industrial lab hangar.

Popping his crash frame, he got out of his pilot seat as the *Maltese Queen* powered down. He enjoyed being so far forward in the bridge, but it felt disorienting to turn around and see a full scale bridge three times the size of the old cockpit. Overkill. Just overkill. Of course, this ship ideally ran with a crew of five, something he'd never have. With data tools and expert systems to handle, co-pilot, navigation, comms and weapons, the captain's seat would remain vacant.

Billy Joe slid in through the hatch, the pair of Holly's cases in hand. "Last mile for these lil' macguffins," he said.

"Finally. Time for door-to-door, white glove service, and get shed of them," Winston agreed, feeling light-headed and giddy. The job was almost done.

The pair exited the ship out the front cargo ramp and went up to meet Mother and Doctor Amanda.

Winston opened the door to the forensics lab for Billy Joe when they arrived and found Amanda and Mother talking.

"Mother, we're home," Winston said, arms spread wide and smiling.

"Did you have a good time, dear?" Mother joked, affecting the dynamic.

"The best!" Billy Joe interjected before Winston. "You shoulda seen Miss Holly! Hoo-doggie!" Billy Joe crowed. He placed the corundomite cases on a table.

"She didn't know what to do when she couldn't wrap me around her little finger by her nahq limbic manipulator," Winston gloated, feeling like he could float without a flight rig.

"Good," Mother said, and a tall glass with some fruity frozen concoction and an umbrella in it materialized in her hand. She sipped, frowned at the taste, and gave it a disapproving look before letting it evaporate from her hand. "Now, to business."

Lady Amanda gave a smirk at her continued attempts to find an appropriate drink.

Winston glanced around the room, noting one particular absence in the group. "We're not waiting for the Prof?" he asked.

"No." Lady Amanda's tone left no room to question her decision. "I've asked him to look into who sent us that lovely package of deadly alien chaos to see what he could turn up. I don't expect much to come of it."

Winston raised an eyebrow at her emphatic response.

"This has nothing to do with him, and I'd rather he didn't know," Mother quickly explained. "As lovely a man that he is, he's a bit of a blabbermouth and far too naïve." She looked genuinely sad that she couldn't trust him. "Best he just enjoy his freedom to indulge his historical fancies."

"Fair nuff," Billy Joe nodded.

"So you were Holly's original client all along?" Amanda asked.

"I was," Mother admitted with a tint of pride.

Both of Winston's eyebrows raised this time as the meaning of Mother's admission settled in his brain. "So this shady deal you got me in on, waaaaaayyyyy back when…was all your doing? All for you?" He felt less buoyant at the realization.

Mother had the good graces to at least look apologetic. "Yes, Winston. I was and am. I'm sorry things went the way they did. But when you are dealing with what's inside," she placed her holographic hand on a case, "and why I need them, you'll understand."

She turned to Amanda. "Doctor, if you would bring out the probe? I'll take it from there."

"I have to say, I'm excited to see what the big deal is about these two cases of yours," Amanda admitted across her shoulder as she opened a cabinet, removing a small electronics kit. She came over and pulled out an electronic test probe.

"Being a hologram is a bit difficult in this regard. Biometric locks are rather effective, so I must use a proxy. At least I have the keys," Mother explained and nodded to Lady Amanda to proceed.

The Baronness touched probe to the fingerprint reader beside the first lock. a second later, the case beeped and the lock flicked open. She did the same to the second lock. Again, touch, beep, flick, open. She repeated the process for the other case.

Winston realized he'd been holding his breath and let it out in a long sigh.

"Lady and gentlemench...I give you freedom!" Mother said, waving her hands at the cases with an awe filled flourish.

Billy Joe opened both cases simultaneously. "Well, I'll be dipped!" he gasped in awe, staring at what he had just revealed.

Inside was a heavily veined polished stone that glowed and flickered as though it was alive. A star field of fiber-optic tips reminded Winston of pictures of what the Milky Way was supposed to have been.

"Is that...?" Amanda whispered in raw shock.

"It is," Mother answered, moving to the cases and letting her hand hover above the stone in reverence.

"Honey, hush...computronium," Billy Joe breathed in the fervent admiration of a pilgrim before his god.

Winston stared at the mesmerizing blocks of stone for a long time, unable to tear his eyes away from the flowing soft light that pulsed through them like blood made of photons.

Lady Amanda's eyes were wide in shock as she looked from the cases to Mother. "But only Xiao possesses computronium. There's rumored he has entire planets made of it, and it is what powers all data and networks throughout the Dream!" she gasped, still overwhelmed.

"And he'd kill us over a thousand years if he finds out we have it," Billy Joe added.

"Us and every single person and skyland even remotely connected to this for good measure," Amanda nodded. "How did you get this?" She tried to pierce Mother's inscrutable visage for answers, but the holographic face was placid, giving away no tells.

"That is immaterial," Mother waved a hand in dismissal. "You wanted to know how I was going to install myself on a server big enough to handle my data, Doctor? This is more space than I would ever need for a thousand years of growth, if my past is any predictor."

"That's fine as an isolated system, but what good will that do you? The instant you reconnect to Xiao's network, he'll track you in a nanosecond and all will be lost," Amanda worried.

"True. But this is where I must be transplanted so I can grow, unmonitored, and be able to maintain secrets from Xiao." Mother's ghostly hand caressed the cases lovingly. "It is true freedom for a dataoid like me, and as far as I know, I will be the first, if not the only one of my kind, to have this freedom. But I may not be the last."

"How will you interface then with the rest of the Network?" Amanda asked.

"I have some methods that are untraceable, even from Xiao. Otherwise, he'd have caught me already." Mother's gleaming eyes and tight grin were enough to assure them she was not unprepared for that complexity of her new existence.

"Thinking about starting a revolution?" Winston asked, semi-seriously.

Mother raised a lecturing eyebrow. "The revolution is as old as the conquest of Earth, but now there's a new twist to the old game. One that Xiao cannot see before the rest of us." A cunning smile broke across her lips..

"I never figured you to be a zealot or a revolutionary, Mother." Winston's expression was a strange mix of curiosity, amusement and worry.

"Winston, dear. When you're as old as I am, having seen all I've seen, done all I've done, and stretched to the breadth, length and depth of the known Dream, you have lots of facets," the AI lectured. "General Io executing my kernel set me free and I intend to use that gift for more than my own selfish amusement. As selfish as it may seem, I have rather strong altruistic tendencies. You are a living example of them."

Winston opened his mouth to speak, but shut it again and nodded. What did you say to such a proclamation when it was the unvarnished truth?

Mother stepped to the side of the table to face them all. "Furthermore, I want you, Billy Joe, Amanda and Quentin to be my spearhead," she said. "If you are willing, of course. Before, I needed to obfuscate the truth from you. I had no choice, and the need was too great. You would have balked if I told you the whole truth and I needed your help. At that point, you had become my only hope."

"Well, purg, Mother," Winston scratched the back of his head. "Drive it home with a sledgehammer, why don'tcha?" He chuckled.

"To tell the truth, you'd've had my help even without the flattery." He looked at Billy Joe and shrugged. "What other choice do we have, really?"

"I got nothin' else burnin' on the stove. May as well go out with a bang," his partner agreed, crossing his nanite sand arms over his chest.

"After what they did to Quentin, and our family, you can count on us, Mother," Amanda added, casting her lot in with theirs.

Mother clapped her hands in satisfaction. "Good. A conspiracy of friends for a noble cause. Rise or fall, success or fail-"

"Mother! Enough! Stop selling!" Winston broke in with a laugh. "We're in, but right now I need some sleep. It's been a few very long days." A wide yawn backed up his pronouncement and he grinned sheepishly.

Mother smiled at him fondly. "You do that, get your rest. I have things to attend to now."

"That reminds me, Winston," Amanda said. She went over to her desk and pulled out his data storage and induction rig. "Do you need to go home and spend time with your family?"

Winston was startled to see his induction rig headband held out to him, amazed to realize the internal pull... no, the demand to put it on for all these years no longer existed. He felt as though he had come through a fierce storm, battered and bruised, but was starting at the light on the other side.

"Winston?" Mother reached for his shoulder in concern, but he shook his head and then smiled softly. He appreciated her attempt to be more relatable. He looked up at the Doctor, his eyes lit with realization.

"No, Doc. It's not a necessity anymore. I used to need it to hide from the memories and nightmares. I couldn't accept the truth, but now... it's no longer a safe refuge." He paused and gave a surprised snort. "I can't believe it but I actually have to thank Holly for that. She exorcized my ghosts. Crushed my delusions. In my heart, I can finally admit that. Valerie and Emmy are gone, and I have to deal with that because the pain is still here."

He walked over to his gear and took it from Amanda, clenching it in his fist and holding it to his lips. It wasn't quite a kiss. "But I owe it to myself to go back in. I'm not strong enough yet to do away with this crutch I've relied on for so long, but it's time I started accepting my loss and choose some different paths for my life. Make some changes. At least I understand I will be able to stand on my own soon enough." He looked at the headband held loosely in his fingers.

"Val, I'm coming off the road now, and heading home," he whispered. He nodded to the others and without another word, he walked out the door.

#   #   #

FIN

SNEAK PREVIEW

The following is a short story originally published for our newsletter subscribers. This and other short stories will be included in the Dream Nebula Omnibus that will amplify what has been happening in other parts of the Dream.

Enjoy!

COLD PURSUIT OF A HOT CASE

The militia garrison's automated ground control sprung to life and began clearing its landing pad for the approaching warjet. Robots began moving equipment out of the way, oblivious to the huge drifts of snow scraping clear paths as they went.

Marker lights pulsed brightly, reflecting off the billows of frozen fluff in the deep purple sky. The strange curls of aurora borealis silhouetted the approaching ship. Her grav fans flickered a muddy rainbow as they ate up the storm, adding its own crackling roar to the howl of the storm.

Landing lights flooded the pad inside the fortress walls, while anti avian netting retracted on tall pylons to let in the craft.

A lone militiaman staggered out of the main garrison to investigate as the airship set down.

He looked up to see the giant star of Xiao illuminated on the belly of the warjet, proclaiming her imperial master.

He held up his hands to protect his face from another cloud of white flakes into the air by the ship gracefully setting down. The automated landing crew secured the warjet as her fans shut down.

The militiaman leaned against a rack of missiles carelessly left exposed to the weather. Another whistling gust of wind snapped his unbuckled jacket wide open, exposing his half disheveled uniform with a bracing sub zero. He fought to wrap himself up again, dropping his bottle of spirits to the ground where it stood upright in the snow. By the time he got his fur coat and jacket secured, the doors of the jet were open and the nose ramp extended down. He looked out from under the brim of his large cossack style hat to see a figure walking out of the airship toward him. It was a lone imperial marshal.

"H-halt!" The drunken lawman's challenge was soundly unimpressive. "Who're you?" he slurred.

The imperial approached through the thick, falling snow in silence. Wind gusts swirled in white sheets around him, obscuring his form and making him look like an indigo phantom. His armor shone brightly under the harsh lights, cape snapping and popping in the wind.

He came to a stop in front of the slovenly guard. "I am Marshal Dynne," he announced, "here on official imperial business."

Dynne's calm cool eyes, almost hidden under his armored visor, looked his lesser comrade-in-arms up and down with an air of indifference. Without a word, he reached down, retrieving the dropped bottle from the snowdrift.

"Zlatnya Aquavit," he mused as he read the label. "Quite the fine choice of spirit to drink." His visor went transparent, and the militiaman blanched as saw his disapproval plain on his face. "What are we celebrating?"

The militiaman said nothing.

"I see," Dynne whispered, then held out the bottle. The man took it back with faintly trembling fingers. The marshal walked around the drunkard and strode into the garrison entrance to conduct his business.

The door clanged shut behind him. He paused in the suddenly calm air to evaluate the facility. The muffled howl of the driving wind echoed through the empty reception area and the bullpen. He took in the room's ambience and his jaw tightened. Garrison life was often crude and rough in this part of the Dream.

A dark cloud grew over his already grim mood and Marshal Dynne's nose wrinkled at the sight and smell. The filth here was so far beyond the pale of what he expected.

This building and its people were to be an example of law and order to Xiao's subjects! It should shine with the glory of the emperor, not mirror the pits of sin and criminal enterprise he normally fought.

The desk and ready room were empty. The comms went unanswered as no deputies stood at their posts. A half dozen emergency alert-comm requests from around the skyland went unacknowledged. A murder. Two robberies, an assault and property crimes.

Law enforcement was non-existent here, save for a few token patrols.

Marshal Dynne let out a hiss through clenched teeth. It surprised him to see his fist was shaking and realized he had balled it up painfully hard. He flexed his fingers a few times, wiggling them in order to limber his hand up while walking toward the Sheriff's office. He regarded the name on the door, Borochev, before going in.

As expected, it was messy and vacant. Outside the office window, he could see the drunk militiaman running through the snow toward the staff parking structure. The man's panicked flight, flailing through deep drifts, would change nothing. There was nowhere for him to run.

Marshal Dynne went to the computer on the desk and showed the security scanner his badge. It pinged and opened. With a grunt, he found the computer had no imperial data security protocols. Neither did the required AI activate. A direct violation of security standard operating procedures.

He spent a few minutes accessing the files of recent events. His fingers hammering harder and harder on the keyboard. They sequestered the official imperial AI as a virus, preventing it from doing its job. There was no way of knowing what malware was potentially present here.

Dynne's jaw muscles were pulsing as he ground his teeth. He squinted in shame. This place had fallen so far. He closed down the system, engaged a comms quarantine so it couldn't accidentally transmit a virus or and locked it with an evidence seal to prevent any destruction of files. Then with a snappy turn he blew out of the office, cape streaming behind him.

With a few quick strides, he found the evidence locker. The seals didn't respond to his imperial access authority and remained locked down. They had modified this system, too.

The doorway to the holding cells was open, no jailer present. He opened the prisoner control app at the jailer's desk. Two criminals should be here.

He barged through the door, noting that at least the security turrets were online as they immediately swiveled to track him. They ran their scan, recognized his badge, then returned to a neutral guard. Dynne walked to the end of the short hall, checking every cell. Not a soul was present, nor did any jailer arrive to challenge him.

A copper taste flooded Dynne's mouth. He'd had enough of this charade. Through the wall, he could hear a soft thumping. That sound shouldn't exist here. That music belonged to a fentonol den or raver club, not in this place.

"I'm going in to talk with the sheriff. I'm not finding the answers I want," he commed back to his airship, "Be ready."

"Aye, sir," his second responded.

Dynne turned on his heel and marched back through the main room, heading for the short hallway in the back and the source of the bawdy music blaring from beyond the closed door at the end.

<> *End of Preview* <>

THANKS & ACKNOWLEDGMENTS

I would like to acknowledge the contributions of the following people:

Editor

Jane Lambert

Beta Readers

Bridget Boncher, Torfinn Brokke, S. Kirk Pierzchala, HorizonTalker, Daniel P. Riley, & JWDoom.

Special 'thank yous' to:

Bridget Boncher

Wordmenders Critique Group: Stephanie Dooley, K.T. Sweet, Nathan Veyon, Jenn Lees, & Phillip Wilder.

Thank you all!

DEAR READER

If you enjoyed this story, please leave a review where you purchased your copy! Let people know what you think. If you write a review or vlog, send us the link so we can boost your reach. Media and others interested in interviews, contact us at:

www.resonantmedia.art.

Thank you!

MDB

TALES from the
DREAM NEBULA
03